THE MYSTERY OF THE LABYRINTHIAN LEGACY

THE THREE INVESTIGATORS

IN

THE MYSTERY OF THE LABYRINTHIAN LEGACY

BY

ELIZABETH ARTHUR & STEVEN BAUER

BASED ON CHARACTERS
CREATED BY ROBERT ARTHUR

Hollow Tree Press 2026

CONTENTS

1

Father Samuel Delivers A Case

The late-summer morning was quiet as Jupiter Jones opened the gate in the fence separating his aunt and uncle's house from the Jones Salvage Yard. A California jay swooped from its perch and landed in front of him, fixing him with a bright eye before pecking at something shiny in the gravel and flying off. Jupiter yawned and stretched.

Ever since he and his friends Pete Crenshaw, Bob Andrews, and Mallory MacLeod had returned from northern California, where they'd solved a case involving the pop star Odetta Dharmapuki and her computer-designer boyfriend Zachary Hughes, everyone, even the birds, had been extremely busy – except for him.

Mallory had been refining her drawings for a new and improved Three Investigators Headquarters they planned to build the following spring; Pete had been frantically finishing a paper for the World History class in which he'd taken an incomplete at the end of their freshman year at Rocky Beach High; and Bob had

been writing up notes for the case he was calling *The Mystery of the Kaleidoscopic Keychain.*

Only Jupiter had had time on his hands. He'd been using it to read a book of essays about human achievements through the ages and to write a long letter to his second cousin Harper. He'd seen her in northern California, and he'd promised her a detailed explanation about how critical thinking pertained to everyday life.

But now he was wondering whether he should also write about intuition. More frequently than Jupiter would once have imagined, a strong intuition about something had ended up helping The Three Investigators solve a case.

That didn't mean that they ignored information and evidence. It simply meant that they also paid attention to their instincts. After all, as Jupiter had decided a long time ago, instinct was often just logical analysis that happened below the level of the conscious mind.

Jupiter was, as always, struck by how chaotic the Salvage Yard was in its surface appearance, and yet how orderly he knew it was in its underlying arrangement. A place for everything and everything in its place wasn't exactly its motto – a lot of stuff got shifted from

one spot to another on a daily basis – but there was never a shortage of ideas about where to put something next.

In fact, Jupiter thought suddenly, the whole place was almost Linnaean in the way it divided things into categories. Big furniture, small furniture, old furniture, elegant architectural gewgaws; they all had their place, and ever since Mallory had started working for Jupiter's aunt and uncle, the categorization had gotten more specific and detailed.

But although Mallory was supposed to arrive later today to work, she wasn't here yet. In fact, at the moment, no one was. Uncle Titus had left early on a buying trip, and Aunt Mathilda had had to go downtown to run some errands. Jupiter was on his way to Headquarters – an old mobile home trailer that had served the firm well during its early years but that he and the other Three Investigators had decided to replace before next summer.

Jupiter had asked Mallory to design the new headquarters, and because they'd be keeping their old one, too, Mallory had suggested they call the original HQ1 and the new one HQ2. Now, as Jupiter made his way through the Salvage Yard, he was struck by how oddly the designations HQ1 and HQ2 suggested that somewhere up ahead of them in the future, there might be an HQ3.

There was no particular reason to think there ever would be, but both the alphabetical system Bob used to title their cases and the mathematical system Mallory had come up with to distinguish their Headquarters had powerful internal logic – allowing people to compare and contrast.

In the book he was reading, one of the essays suggested that comparing and contrasting things was the fundamental business of the human mind, and Jupiter thought there was a lot of truth to that. He was about to walk through the outdoor workshop toward Easy Three – the entrance to HQ1 – when the UPS truck rattled into the yard.

Ever since his Aunt Mathilda had hired Mallory to describe and photograph objects that could be sold on the Jones Salvage Yard website, Billy Wells had been coming almost daily to pick up packages Aunt Mathilda was sending to customers all over the United States. But that wasn't why he was here today.

As usual, Billy – who Jupiter still called Mr. Wells – was wearing brown shorts and a brown button-down short-sleeved shirt. His sunglasses were pushed high up on his forehead as he jumped down from the driver's seat, a box in his hand.

"Jupiter!" he said. "What do you have for me today?"

"Nothing that I know of, Mr. Wells," he said. "My aunt didn't mention any pick-ups."

"Righty-o," Billy said. "There's just this then." He handed the package to Jupiter. "It's for you. At least it's your name on the label."

Jupiter took the package and stared down at it in amazement.

"That was fast!" he said. "Thanks!"

"Have a great day," Billy said. He jumped into his truck, backed up, and zoomed away before Jupiter even had a chance to properly say goodbye.

Well, this was a surprise. Since they'd gotten back to Rocky Beach from northern California, Jupiter had been planning, together with Pete and Bob, a surprise end-of-the-season present for Mallory.

Several cases back, Jupiter had decided it was time to put her name on The Three Investigators' business card, and Pete and Bob had agreed. When they'd first established The Three Investigators, they'd designed and printed their card on an old letterpress they'd found in the Salvage Yard and fixed up, and

11

they'd kept using it until last summer.

This time they'd decided to use a modern printing service. The cards would be slightly larger so that Mallory's name would fit on them easily, and they'd be ready to pick up the following day, with Mallory's name and the words "Special Consultant" printed in what seemed to be her favorite color – a deep blue-green she called teal.

Since Jupiter, Pete, and Bob wanted Mallory to finally feel like a full member of the firm, they'd also decided to give her a new bike helmet and her own chalk – and these were what had just arrived. Since Jupiter didn't want Mallory to stumble across them by accident before the day came to actually give them to her, he decided to take the package back to his house and put it in his bedroom.

Once there, Jupiter opened the box and took out the helmet and chalk. The helmet was just like his and Pete's and Bob's – the same sleek design, the same fiberglass – but once again in the deep blue-green color. He thought she'd look great in it, with her shoulder-length red hair. As for the chalk, it matched the color of the helmet pretty well – as he saw when he held a piece against the fiberglass.

Satisfied, Jupiter put the chalk back,

tucked the helmet into its box, and put both of them on a shelf in his closet. Now, if the cards also turned out well, The Three Investigators and their Special Consultant would really be in business!

Jupiter was once more headed for HQ1 when a light gray van pulled through the wrought-iron entrance gates. It looked like the kind that was usually used for transporting small groups belonging to some organization or other.

Although the windows were tinted, and Jupiter couldn't see inside, it had sliding doors on both sides and he guessed that there were four rows of seats that could easily fit eight to ten people. But there was no sign on the door to indicate the nature of its business, so Jupiter was startled when the driver's door opened and a priest clambered down onto the gravel.

At least Jupiter thought he must be a priest. He was used to seeing clergy wearing a priest's collar, but this older man was wearing a black cassock, with a row of black buttons from his neck to his waist where the garment was fastened by a black cord. It was so long that it seemed to sweep across the gravel as the man approached him. He had a kindly, somewhat bemused expression; his white hair was in need of a cut; and his black glasses made him look a bit owlish. Jupiter's first thought was that he must be lost.

"Can I help you?" Jupiter asked.

"I hope so, young man," the priest said. "I'm looking for a detective firm that calls itself The Three Investigators and is headed by a person with the singular name of Jupiter Jones. I was told that his Headquarters was somewhere in this Salvage Yard."

If Jupiter had been startled before, he was even more startled now.

"I'm Jupiter Jones," he said. "My colleagues aren't here at the moment, but I'd be happy to talk with you myself."

The priest smiled at the news and then looked a bit dejected. "I'm afraid it's complicated," he said.

"Most of our cases are. Take all the time you want," Jupiter reassured him.

"My name is Father Samuel," the man said. "As you can see" – he looked down at the vestments he was wearing – "I'm a Roman Catholic priest. No longer practicing. When I turned seventy, it was time for me to retire. So I'm living with some other retired priests in a home provided by the diocese, on the edge of Rocky Beach."

"Do you have a problem you need help with?" Jupiter asked politely.

The priest looked alarmed. "No!" he said. "Not exactly. Well, now that you mention it, yes." His face reddened, a sharp contrast to his white hair. "I'm here hoping to help a friend. Two friends, actually."

It seemed to Jupiter that the priest had a problem answering a direct question.

"The names of my friends are Jacob Suleiman," the priest said, "and his son, Adam. Who is about your age, I think. Jacob is an architect who lives in the Bay Area, but it's really Adam who sent me here. He asked specially that The Three Investigators be called in. In order to solve the mystery of something that just happened to him and his father."

He looked at Jupiter uncertainly. "Is there somewhere we could go to – " he lowered his voice almost to a whisper – "talk?"

"Certainly," Jupiter said. "I'm afraid Three Investigators' Headquarters is under renovation at the moment, but we can at least sit in the shade somewhere. Why don't you come with me?"

He led the man to The Three Investigators' outdoor workshop, which, now that he looked at it, was not the most auspicious place to entertain a new client. Several of the boys' projects, in various stages of completion, covered the workbenches, and the green metal chairs were old and not very comfortable.

He felt slightly embarrassed. The time had clearly come for them to have a proper meeting place so that visitors like Father Samuel could be made comfortable as they consulted. He was glad that Mallory's plans were nearing completion, and that by the beginning of the following investigative season, their new headquarters would be up and running.

Father Samuel's robes swished over the gravel as he followed Jupiter. He gathered them around him as he lowered himself, rather awkwardly, into one of the chairs and sat without speaking until Jupiter nudged him by asking him to say more about the Suleimans.

But instead of answering Jupiter's question, Father Samuel began talking about himself.

"When I was a young priest," he said, "I had a parish of my own in California – to the north of here, in the Bay area – and I enjoyed it very much. But I became restless, and when I was in my late 40s, I was selected by my diocese to go on missions to countries where there were very few Christians in proportion to the rest of the population."

Jupiter couldn't yet understand what this had to do with the problem that had brought Father Samuel to the Salvage Yard, but he didn't interrupt.

"Among other places," Father Samuel continued, "I was sent to Morocco, in northern Africa. A marvelous country, but one in which only about one per cent – one percent! – of the population was Christian. Naturally, I met other Catholics while I was there, and one I became friends with was a man by the name of Daniel Suleiman – Jacob Suleiman's father. I also became friends with Jacob himself. He was just a young man, then – some twenty years younger than he is now – but already an excellent architect."

Jupiter's interest perked. It seemed the old man was circling the real story. "So you met the friend on whose behalf you are here to-day many years ago in North Africa," he said encouragingly, hoping this would focus the priest.

Father Samuel's eyes brightened. "Yes," he said. "Exactly." He went on to explain that the Suleiman family had long been Catholic, even though it had deep roots in a part of the world that was overwhelmingly Muslim.

The priest said there was a good deal of anti-Christian sentiment in Morocco and northern Africa in general − though the family had not been affected by it. At least not until young Jacob fell in love with an Arab Muslim woman named Zahra. To honor her soon-to-be husband, Zahra decided to convert to Catholicism, but since this would have caused a lot of problems with her family, just after they were married Jacob and Zahra immigrated to northern California.

"That was about eighteen years ago now," Father Samuel said. "Jacob became a successful architect in the Bay Area, where he used his skills to design houses that had a strong Moroccan influence but were somehow also distinctly Californian. He designed and built the house he and Zahra lived in as an example of what he could do."

"Did you have anything to do with their coming to California?" Jupiter asked.

Father Samuel smiled modestly. "I think so," he said. "I told them many stories about California, and especially about the Bay area. And I returned to the state not long after Jacob and Zahra had built their house."

But the story turned tragic very quickly. Jacob and Zahra had a son about two years after they were settled in California, the priest told Jupiter – a son they named Adam – and two years later, when Adam was still an infant, Zahra had died of cancer.

"It was very sad," Father Samuel said, shaking his head mournfully. "Jacob stopped going to Mass and little by little he stopped believing. How could the God he had known all his life have allowed his wife to die? Jacob never remarried but poured all his passion and energy into taking care of Adam – into educating him and helping him follow his own interests.

"And he has done a wonderful job," Father Samuel added. "Adam is an extremely engaging young man. And in the last few years the son – though not the father – has started going to church again. Although he's been going to an Episcopalian church, not a Catholic one. He attends the Grace Cathedral in San Francisco."

The priest smiled sweetly.

"This is all very interesting," Jupiter said. "And I'm very sorry to hear about Mrs. Suleiman. But you still haven't told me how The Three Investigators might be helpful to Mr. Suleiman and Adam."

Father Samuel sighed. "I was never very

good at getting to the point," the priest confessed. "You must forgive me. Let me get down to it then. When Jacob and his wife first came to California, they brought an extensive library with them – a library that contained any number of very old and important Catholic texts and other memorabilia. It's actually about an item in this collection that Adam wants his father to consult with you and your companions."

At last! Jupiter thought.

"Was the item stolen?" he asked.

"Ah," the priest said. "That's a difficult question. It was and it wasn't. Yes and no. Sort of stolen – but not very successfully."

Jupiter frowned. The priest wasn't making much sense. "Have they reported the loss to anyone else?" he asked.

"Yes, of course," the priest said. "To the Alameda police."

"Oh," Jupiter said, surprised. "They live up in Alameda?"

"Didn't I mention that?" the priest asked. "I meant to mention that."

"No," Jupiter said. "No, you didn't."

"But I did say something about Jacob being an architect in the Bay Area, didn't I?" the priest said, suddenly agitated. "Oh, dear. I'm making quite a mess of this. But yes! That's why Adam called me and asked if I would come here today and convince The Three Investigators to take the case. It would have taken them six hours to drive here, and I was less than a half hour away, and they trusted me to convey the urgency."

Urgency? Jupiter thought. Conveying urgency, he noted, was perhaps not what the priest was best at.

However, he was starting to get the suspicion that at the end of this long-winded tale something provocative and interesting must lie. Something seemed to have been stolen and not stolen at the same time, and although The Three Investigators had been involved in any number of cases concerning missing objects, there never had been one about which *that* could be said.

He thought he'd continue to try to prod the priest to give up his secret, which he seemed both eager and reluctant to divulge.

"So Mr. Suleiman and his son have had something of a religious nature stolen from them and would like The Three Investigators to get it back?"

"Well, not exactly," the priest said.

Jupiter was getting frustrated. "Well, what *do* they want? And why would they even have heard about us? Why would they think that we are the proper investigative firm to consult, especially when we live six hours away from San Francisco?"

"It's because of Adam, really," the priest said. "You see, about a year ago, Adam discovered The Three Investigators' website, which he has followed ever since. He's read all of the case reports written by your colleague Bob Andrews, and he's been very impressed. Very impressed."

Father Samuel nodded his head thoughtfully, took off his glasses, and wiped them on the sleeve of his cassock, then put them back on. In the time they were off his face, Jupiter noticed that the priest's eyes were a milky blue, watery, and very timid. He smiled at Jupiter feebly.

"I'm very pleased to hear that," he told Father Samuel. "And Bob will be especially pleased. He works very hard on the case reports, and he'll be excited to hear that something has come our way as a direct result of his work."

Actually, Jupiter knew that Bob would be more than pleased. He'd be ecstatic. All summer, he'd been hoping that someone with a mystery or conundrum to solve would visit their website and read Bob's case reports. But they'd now gone through an entire summer season – five whole cases – and not a single case had come to them in that way. Three of their cases had been more or less accidental and two had been brought to them by people The Three Investigators already knew.

As Jupiter thought this out, he sat and stared expectantly at Father Samuel, but once again, the priest seemed to have come to a stop. Jupiter decided he would simply ask.

"So what is it that was stolen, exactly?"

The priest looked almost frightened for a moment, and then his expression settled down and he became very solemn.

"Poems," he said. "Great poems."

Although Jupiter, Pete, and Bob had recently solved a case that involved a novel that had gone missing twenty years before, they'd never been involved with the actual theft of a literary work.

"Poems?" he asked, to keep the old man going.

"Yes," Father Samuel said, a pained expression on his face. "Twelve villanelles written by the distinguished French poet Jacques de Boissy, who lived during the Renaissance and contemplated the mysteries of the labyrinth at the Cathedral of our Lady of Chartres. The villanelles are sublime, transporting. Just reading them would turn a reader into a believer. And these are not copies. These are the original handwritten final drafts – the only ones in the world."

Here, Father Samuel stopped and looked at Jupiter, hoping he had conveyed the import of his information.

"The portfolio also contained twelve English translations done by a man named Wilfred Willoughby – an English poet who lived in the 1700s," he added.

Jupiter was pretty sure he'd heard of the French cathedral, but he'd never heard of Jacques de Boissy or Willoughby – and since he had no idea what a villanelle was, he wished that either Bob or Mallory were with him. It was possible that one of *them* knew.

However, he was on his own at the moment, so he said, "What's a villanelle? And tell me more about this labyrinth."

He hoped the priest would be better at answering direct questions, and, in fact, he was. As Father Samuel slowly picked up steam and told him the whole story, Jupiter felt his scalp tingle. It seemed that the thief had taken a portfolio from the Suleimans' library not long after Jacob had focused his attention on the fact that he owned the only copies in existence written in the hand of the poet himself. When he learned this, he'd decided he should make a gift of them to a religious center, The Tri-Faith Center for the Study of the Abrahamic Religions, and when it was stolen instead, he feared he would never be able to do that.

But two days after the portfolio had disappeared from the Suleimans' home, a cleaning woman working for Grace Cathedral found the portfolio on a pew – apparently untouched and unharmed.

The cleaning woman had taken the portfolio to the Lost and Found, but the person who ran the Lost and Found had opened it up, seen it was something special, and taken it to the dean of the cathedral.

The dean happened to have read in the San Francisco *Chronicle* about the portfolio and how it had been stolen just before it was to be donated to the Tri-Faith Center. He therefore called Jacob Suleiman and returned it.

"And the poems were all there and unharmed?" Jupiter asked Father Samuel.

"The twelve poems were untouched," Father Samuel said. "But the portfolio itself had been slightly damaged. It's made of Moroccan leather and is hundreds of years old."

In a burst of sudden clarity, the priest went on, "Someone had picked apart the stitching at the top of the back cover, revealing what you might call a secret pocket – a hiding place. It seems the thief wasn't after the poems at all but something else that had been hidden in the portfolio. Adam is absolutely convinced that something very important must have been stolen. He's also convinced that whoever stole the portfolio knew what he or she was after. The fact that the portfolio was left in a place where no harm would come to it – and where the thief knew it would end up being returned to the rightful owners – seems to Adam proof of his hypothesis."

For a moment, Jupiter tried to keep himself from smiling, but when he couldn't, he found himself grinning broadly. This was totally new ground for The Three Investigators, and Jupiter thought the probability was high that it was going to turn into something very interesting indeed.

Of course, it would mean making arrangements for The Three Investigators and Mallory to travel to San Francisco as soon as possible, but even though there were only two weeks left in the summer before school started, and they'd have to solve the case quickly, if it panned out it would be a fitting end to a satisfying season – and Jupiter was happy to think that it would be as a result of Bob's good work. In fact, he could hardly wait to get the rest of Father Samuel's story, then get on the phone to Bob.

2

High Excitement

At that moment, Bob was sitting at the table on the outdoor patio of his house's small back yard, finishing a bowl of cereal and talking with his father as the morning light streamed through the eucalyptus trees. The night before, Bob had completed his report on The Three Investigators' most recent case and had uploaded it to their website. For some reason, he felt particularly pleased with this one.

Across from him, his father folded the morning edition of the paper he wrote for – the Los Angeles *Sun* – and placed it aside.

"Did you have a chance to read the new case report?" Bob asked eagerly. "I know I just gave it to you last night, but – "

"Indeed I did," his father said, smiling. "I was just about to say so. It was excellent as always. It sounds like a rousing adventure. I'm glad I only know about these cases of yours after they're concluded, or I'd be worried a lot of the time. I found the stuff about the Wiccan coven particularly interesting."

"Thanks," Bob said. "I keep hoping the

reports will lead to new cases, but so far I haven't had much luck in that department. I was thinking maybe we ought to advertise on social media, to get more people to look at the website."

As Bob's father picked up his coffee cup, his eyes held the look they always had when he was about to dispense parental wisdom.

"Did I tell you about Hal Winshall?" he asked.

Bob looked at his father shrewdly. "No," he said, "but I get the feeling that you're about to."

Mr. Andrews laughed. "Hal is a friend of mine at the *Sun*," Mr. Andrews said. "I've known him for years. He has a column that covers cultural and political trends. Anyway, he recently wrote a mild-mannered column about the divisiveness of identity politics, and wouldn't you know it? The social media mob came for him. They denounced him and bullied him and called for him to be fired. Fortunately the paper stood by him, but other people, as you know, haven't been so lucky. These social media mobs are a menace."

"I agree with you," Bob said. "Mobs of any kind are a menace. Still, what do you think of my idea? Social media of some kind might be a way for The Three Investigators to let the world know about us. We could have joined X and Facebook almost two years ago. You only have to be thirteen and we're all almost fifteen now. I'm just starting to get a little frustrated about how few people seem to have bumped into my case reports while they're surfing around the Internet."

"I suppose there are good arguments to be made for social media," Mr. Andrews said, "but it does present a lot of opportunities for bad behavior and terrible writing. It's also chaotic. People's comments and questions are always flying around as if they've exploded from a box."

"That may be true," Bob said, "but this summer we haven't gotten a single case that came from readers."

"But I thought you'd gotten a lot of inquiries," his father said.

"We have," Bob said, "but none of them ever led to an actual case. The same thing happened last summer. Only one case had anything to do with my reports, but though Daman Dulwalia *did* find us online, I don't think he would have followed through on contacting us if it hadn't been for Califia García-Williams telling him she knew us."

"I know how you must feel," Mr. Andrews said. "But it has nothing to do with the quality of your writing. You're really very talented, and your mother and I agree you have a bright future as a journalist or historian – or even as a fiction writer."

"Thanks, Dad," Bob said. "That really cheers me up."

"Well, I've got to get ready for work," Mr. Andrews said, gathering his dishes to take to the kitchen. "But don't worry. The world will find you eventually."

Bob followed his father to the kitchen and then went up to his bedroom, thinking about their conversation. He still wasn't convinced that social media was all bad, and he suddenly wondered if anyone that he, Jupiter, and Pete had met over their last eleven cases had an active X account. Maybe a quick investigation would give him information he could use to make a decision.

He knew you could check out someone's X's account without having one of your own, so he started to go through a list he quickly made of everyone they'd met in the course of their cases. The first person was Isabella Chang, who'd been their client in their very first case of the previous summer, but he didn't even bother to look her up. She was in her 80s and her eyesight was so bad she couldn't really use a computer. Wally Tate, who lived with Isabella and was in his 90s, surely didn't have an account either.

Bob also knew that Phillipa Paxton and Rafael Solares didn't use X, and he assumed that Lyle Smith didn't either – he checked and found that he was right – but Lyle's partner Cornelius Patterson, an art restorer, did.

Cornelius only had about 300 followers. He didn't post much, and he clearly used the account mostly to help him get work. So that was important information. Thinking of art made Bob check out Connor O'Malley, their artist friend up in Auburn – who, as it turned out, had an X account with about 800 followers. It occurred to Bob that artists must be using X as a kind of publicity.

He checked out the actor Per Jorgensen, who didn't seem to have an account. That didn't surprise Bob. Per was older and had already been very successful before the technology appeared. And, for an actor, he was really pretty private. Then Bob thought of the two real stars they'd met – Daman Duwalia and Odetta Dharmapuki.

It turned out that Daman had a million

and a half followers and Odetta had almost two million! Amazing. It was hard to imagine having that many people eager to hear whatever you had to say. In fact, Bob was sure he wouldn't like that. It would be much too much responsibility – and might wind up making you think you were a lot more important than you really were, he thought.

Finally he thought of Ivan Fedorov and his wife Cassandra – an actor/musician and a poet. They both had accounts, but Ivan had only about three thousand followers and Cassandra had fewer than two hundred. It seemed to Bob that, if you were already famous for something, like Daman and Odetta were, then you immediately had millions of followers, but if you were just starting out, like Connor or Ivan or Cassandra, it was hard to get people to follow you.

In that case, maybe it *wouldn't* make sense for The Three Investigators to open social media accounts as a way to get better known. Maybe it would just be a waste of time and an aggravation in the end.

Though Bob felt momentarily discouraged, he remembered that the cases they *had* gotten in the last two summers had been great. Even if they never got another case because of his case reports, it would be O.K. with him, since word of mouth had brought them dependably intriguing and exciting work – which was what mattered, after all. The reports were important as history. And, he hoped – thinking about what his father had said – maybe as literature, too!

Besides, it was kind of nice that they didn't have a new case pressing on them right at the moment. It wouldn't be *that* bad to take a break before their sophomore year in high school started.

However, just then his cellphone rang. It was Jupiter. Bob punched 'accept' and said, "Hey, Jupe. What's going on?"

Jupiter sounded keyed up. "A really unusual case," he said. "It's too complicated to go into all of it now, but you should get over here as soon as you can. I think you're going to be really pleased."

Instantly Bob forgot everything he'd been thinking about having some time off. A new case! He rushed around his room grabbing his things – the cellphone, the black zippered case he kept Three Investigators papers in, his laptop.

"Hey Dad," he yelled as he made for the front door. "I'm off to the Salvage Yard. Jupe just called. We've got a new case!"

In no time, he'd put on his helmet and his bicycle clips and was shooting down the streets of Rocky Beach toward the Jones Salvage Yard. Ten minutes later he pulled up in front of the Office where he found Jupiter pacing back and forth, his hands clasped behind his back.

"Ah," he said. "You're here! I haven't been able to reach Pete or Mallory yet, but I want to get started. The case isn't exactly urgent, but it's one I really want to take, and we don't have much time to get it solved before we have to start getting ready for the new school year."

He hurried off toward Headquarters, with Bob beside him.

"This is a case I think you'll be pleased to hear about," Jupiter told him. "Our client is a fifteen-year-old boy named Adam Suleiman who absolutely insisted that his father Jacob call on the services of The Three Investigators – solely because of your case reports! He found the website about a year ago, has read every single one of your reports, and says he knows we're the people he needs."

Bob was almost speechless. If he'd only known this earlier, he wouldn't have spent so much time thinking about X!

"Have you met Adam?" Bob asked.

"No," Jupiter said. "A friend of his father – a priest named Father Samuel, who lives in Rocky Beach – showed up at the Salvage Yard this morning. Adam and his father actually live up north, in Alameda."

"So what's the case?" Bob asked.

"Just wait a sec, and I'll show you when we get into HQ1."

It was funny, Bob thought, but they'd all already started to talk about their first and only Headquarters as if the second one was already built! Jupiter opened Easy Three and ushered Bob through the door.

Inside Headquarters, Bob immediately saw the new computer and display given to them as a thank you for solving their most recent case. Three days after they'd gotten back from northern California – where they'd helped a computer whiz named Zachary Hughes get to the bottom of a case of electronic harassment and blackmail – the desktop computer, printer and copier, and large digital display had arrived. It had been a huge surprise. The computer dwarfed the desk and made the interior of Headquarters feel even more cramped, but it was also cheerful and beautiful – and very

very fast!

Jupiter had never been all that fond of computers, but ever since this new one had arrived, he'd seemed much more interested in spending time on it than he had with the old one. Bob saw that he'd opened several browser windows simultaneously and that they were flared across the display like a sheaf of papers.

Jupiter sat down and so did Bob, and as Jupiter grabbed the mouse and the keyboard, he explained what he'd been looking at. One window was open to the website for a place called the Tri-Faith Center for the Study of the Abrahamic Religions.

As Bob studied the computer screen, Jupiter said, "To answer your question, it appears that a portfolio of twelve 15th-century poems by a Frenchman named Jacques de Boissy was stolen from the Suleimans' house just before Jacob was about to make a gift of it to a religious studies center. They're the only copies in the world written in the poet's own hand. A few days later, the portfolio was abandoned with all the poems inside it in a cathedral in San Francisco."

"That doesn't really answer my question though, does it?" Bob asked, smiling.

"Adam thinks something that he and his

father never even knew was in the portfolio had been taken before it was left in the cathedral. He wants us to try to determine what was taken and – presumably – to get it back." Now it was Jupiter who was smiling, and Bob could see that he was quite excited at the thought of such a novel challenge.

"O.K.," Bob said. "What are the poems about?"

"Father Samuel had a little trouble describing their actual content," Jupiter told him, "though they're clearly devotional poems – religious poems. He's a somewhat vague man – or at least he appeared to me to be one. But he did say the poems were written by de Boissy while he contemplated a very famous labyrinth which had been inlaid in stone in the floor of the Cathedral of Chartres. Do you want to see it?"

"Sure," said Bob. Jupiter brought another browser window to the fore – this one displaying the labyrinth in Chartres Cathedral. It was a perfect circle inside of which was an intricate design – geometrically complex, a series of eleven circles that led one to the next, to the center, where there was a sort of six-petaled rose. Bob wasn't religious, but the design of the labyrinth was both beautiful and inspiring, Bob thought.

The fact was, up until he'd seen this photograph, he'd always thought of a labyrinth as something tortuous and unpleasant – or at the very least confusing – but in reality, this design, although complex, was also straightforward, simple, and very peaceful.

"Here's the way you get into it," Jupiter said, pointing to an open space in the circle's circumference. "If you enter there and then keep walking, never crossing the solid lines, you eventually get to the very center. It seems that the labyrinth symbolizes the pilgrim's journey toward God and was constructed based on the principles of what they call sacred geometry."

"Sacred geometry!" exclaimed Bob. "That reminds me of our first case of the summer, and all that Freemason stuff about God being the Great Geometrician. Or was it the Great Architect?"

"I think it was both," Jupiter said. "Anyway, the Chartres labyrinth was constructed in the early 1200s, and since then it's been reproduced a number of times in other locations around the world."

"Really?" Bob asked.

"Yes, really," said Jupiter. "And guess what? The finest reproduction anywhere on the planet is in the floor of the Grace Cathedral in San Francisco!"

Bob got a chill. "Where the portfolio was abandoned?"

"Exactly," said Jupiter. "And also where Adam Suleiman goes to church. Here's the Grace Cathedral website."

Jupiter moved the website for Chartres to the side and enlarged a window which was loaded with the website of Grace Cathedral in San Francisco. The cathedral was Episcopal, not Catholic – though it had a very traditional look about it, at least on the outside, Bob thought. But when Jupiter opened a picture of the Grace Cathedral labyrinth and set it side by side with the labyrinth in Chartres, he was astounded. Wow! he thought. Just wow!

"So let me make sure I've got this straight," he said to Jupiter, still staring at the labyrinths. "Jacob and Adam Suleiman owned the original handwritten versions of twelve poems written in the 15th century about the labyrinth on the left, and Adam now goes to the church with the reproduction labyrinth. That's really strange. What was a thief doing in the cathedral to begin with? And why would he leave the portfolio there?"

"That's what I want to know," Jupiter

said. "The cleaning woman took the portfolio to the Lost and Found, but when the dean of the cathedral. saw it, he called Jacob Suleiman and returned it. Adam is convinced that something very important must have been stolen."

"So what do you think it was?" Bob asked.

"That," Jupiter said, "is what we're going to have to find out. The thief must have known not only that there *was* this so-called secret pocket, but also what was in it. And if he or she could know, we have a very good chance of finding out – either by tracking him down and finding out from him, or by finding out first and then tracking him down."

"It won't be easy," Bob said. "Especially since we have no idea what we're looking for."

"That's true," Jupiter said. "But when we were on the case of the Galilean grindstone, I remember talking about the fact that most criminals are stupid. Well, this one probably isn't – and *that* should help us find him! The only thing I'm worried about is time. School starts soon, and it looks like we'll have to get ourselves up to the Bay Area. Which could be a problem in itself.

"As I'm sure you know, San Francisco and the area around it has changed a lot since the days you ended up there in the case concerning the Green family," Jupiter went on. "It's even changed since the four of us went to the opening of the Frémont Exhibit – less than a year ago. A lot of stores are closing because people keep coming in and stealing things, and a lot of buildings are standing vacant. There's a lot of crime and very little punishment."

"I know, said Bob. "I was actually talking with my mother about that the other day. After they got out of China, via Hong Kong, her parents ended up living in San Francisco. My mother was born there, and she says it's a totally different place these days. I think we should find somewhere to stay that isn't actually in the city."

"I agree," said Jupiter. "But I'm also having trouble getting in touch with Mallory. I called Mr. Crenshaw earlier and he told me Pete was at the library working on that history paper he never finished. He has to turn it in by August 20th if he wants to take another history class this year."

"He'll get it done," Bob said. "When Pete sets his mind to something, nothing can stop him."

"I called Miss Bennett at the library," Jupiter said, "and asked her to tell Pete to get over here as soon as he's done. But where's Mallory? She's not answering her phone and I thought she was coming to work at the Salvage Yard today. We've got to get organized!"

Bob could see that Jupiter was getting agitated. Though he was clearly excited about the challenge of finding something when he didn't even know what it was, he also didn't particularly like the pressure of knowing their investigations would have to stop when the new school year began.

As for Mallory, there were a lot of reasons she might not be answering her phone, but when she got to the Salvage Yard, Bob knew she was going to love the pictures of the labyrinth at Grace Cathedral — and the labyrinth itself, once they got there. Given how much she loved interesting buildings, the whole thing should be totally up her alley. It should also be up his — because, just like the case involving Ivan Fedorov's grandfather, this case, too, involved the work of a famous writer.

But just as Bob was about to say this, Jupiter — who had been poking around on the Internet in a way that wasn't really typical of him — suddenly said, "Uh-oh. As if it weren't bad enough to have San Francisco falling apart more drastically every day, it seems that another one of those protest groups – not the one we ran into last summer, but another one – has been moving around the Bay area looking for things about the past they can protest – or destroy!

"We'd better not stay in Sausalito," Jupiter continued. "It seems this group is trying to get a World War One memorial in the middle of Sausalito taken down by the city – even though all it says is 'In Loving Memory of the Sons of Sausalito Who Gave Their Lives In The World War 1914-1918.' At the bottom of the plaque are the words 'Dedicated By Their Comrades Who Came Back.' How could anyone object to that?"

"People seem able to object to anything," Bob said. "And they really like making chaos out of order."

"I know they do," said Jupiter grimly. "And given how dirty and crime-ridden and chaotic San Francisco has been getting in recent years, I'm suddenly wondering whether or not we should actually go there – especially so close to the start of the new school year."

"We'll be careful. *Really* careful," Bob said reassuringly.

Still, he knew that when it came to making decisions about what The Three Investigators should risk, Jupiter tended to be pretty conservative. For a moment, Bob felt worried that he might pull the plug on the whole idea, but luckily Jupiter said, "I agree. We will," – and when he added "I can only hope that will be enough," Bob decided to focus on the first sentiment rather than the second!

3

One Kind of Plan Leads To Another

At the dining table in her apartment in the Wessex House, Mallory sat staring down at her plans for the new Three Investigators Headquarters. Her chin rested on her palm. She was glad to have the apartment to herself this morning, and although she'd told Jupiter and his Aunt Mathilda that she'd be in to do some work at the Salvage Yard later, for now she'd turned off her phone and was focused on the task at hand.

She was feeling pressure to get the plans for HQ2 done by August 20th so that she could present them formally to Jupiter, Pete, and Bob before school started. She'd done some good work at the beginning of the summer, but their case up in Auburn had put a crimp in her hope to get the project done early.

Luckily, over the last three days, she'd not only had a lot of free time but also a burst of creativity. Her mind had been flooded with ideas, and she'd managed to get them all down on paper. There was so much noise in the world, she thought, and working intently on a project really focused the mind.

What Mallory wanted for HQ2 was a high hip roof, with four roof planes and a long narrow dormer built into each quadrant. At the apex, she'd planned a cupola with a light in it, which at night would shine like a beacon in all four directions. Mallory thought of the cupola as a sort of mini-lighthouse that would remind them of the lighthouse that had been so important to a case in Santa Barbara earlier that summer.

During that case she and the others had discussed the interesting fact that Jupiter, Bob, Pete, and she had been born under four subsequent signs of the zodiac — signs that signified Fire, Earth, Air, and Water, the four elements that made up the universe, according to the ancient Greeks.

Now, she planned to mount rectangular wooden plaques on the four sides of the cupola, with the names of the four elements carved into the wood. Jupiter's element — fire — would face the main entrance, with Bob's, Pete's, and hers going around the cupola clockwise — and over the main door would be another plaque, this one curved, with the words The Three Investigators, and under it, tucked into the curve, their chimera logo.

But although Mallory also had a lot of almost-completed ideas for how to organize and finish the inside space, when she looked at her watch she saw that it was well past time for her to get over to the Salvage Yard. She gathered up the plans tapped them purposefully on the dining room table. Then she picked up her pencils and ruler and eraser and carried them and the plans to her bedroom where she set them squarely on top of the immigrant's chest the boys had given her the summer before, and which remained one of her most cherished possessions.

She had to move the rubber model of the Loch Ness monster she'd won the summer before at a camp for Scottish music and dance off to the side. For the time being, Mallory set Nessie on her desk – right next to a carved wooden raven that a boy named Jimmy Little-wolf had given her at the end of a recent case. She'd really liked Jimmy, but since he went to Palisade Point High School and didn't live in Rocky Beach, she doubted she'd see him any time soon. Which was too bad, in a way. She and he had a lot in common.

Mallory gathered her belongings and locked the apartment. Outside, she unchained her bike, put on her helmet, and took off. She found she wasn't in a huge hurry. In fact, she was luxuriating in having some unscheduled time. She was sure she wasn't the only one who could use a break. The summer, with its five cases − three of which had taken them away from Rocky Beach − had been a whirlwind.

She was daydreaming about carefully copying her plans onto new sheets of paper to make them perfect and then putting them into the portfolio she'd already bought for their presentation. As she lazily drifted through the Salvage Yard's wrought-iron gates, she was imagining the looks on the boys' faces when she showed them her plans.

She'd barely come to a stop when she heard Jupiter's agitated voice. "Mallory!" he called. "Where have you been?"

Jupiter and Bob were coming toward her in a hurry from the outdoor workshop, and the expressions on their faces were a far cry from what she'd imagined. Both Jupiter and Bob were in a state of high excitement. Jupiter, who was usually calm and methodical, couldn't seem to keep his hands at his sides.

"We were getting worried," Bob said. "You always answer your phone."

"I know," Mallory said. "I just turned it off for a while this morning because I wanted to concentrate on what I was doing."

"Well, you're here at last," Jupiter said, "though I'm not sure you're going to have time to get any work done for Aunt Mathilda today."

"What's going on?" she asked.

"We've got a new case," Bob said. "Up in the Bay Area. You're going to love it. It's got labyrinths and cathedrals and poems and a criminal Jupiter thinks must be pretty smart. Or at least out of the ordinary. A fifteen-year-old boy named Adam Suleiman wants to hire us because of my case reports!"

"That's great!" Mallory said, smiling at Bob in what she hoped was a congratulatory manner. Her mind whirled as she stood listening while Jupiter and Bob almost tripped over one another trying to fill her in on the details. Gradually the outlines became clear. Someone had stolen a leather portfolio of twelve medieval poems and then abandoned it in a San Francisco cathedral after taking an unknown something out of a secret pocket.

"A secret pocket?" Mallory said. "I love secret pockets. What cathedral was the portfolio left in? And why was it left there? Isn't San Francisco getting really dangerous? I read that some famous tech guy was stabbed to death

50

outside his car just the other day. There was also a kidnapping where a ten-year-old girl was held for ransom!"

"The Suleimans live in Alameda," Jupiter said.

"But the portfolio showed up on Nob Hill in San Francisco," Bob said. "In a pew in Grace Cathedral. A great Gothic cathedral Adam Suleiman is now attending."

Mallory nodded and thought for a minute. "If the poems are so valuable, why didn't the thief just keep them and sell them? Or hold *them* for ransom or something?" she asked.

"That's one of the things we have to find out," Jupiter said. "To be honest, that's actually why I'm so eager to get on this case. Many of the details don't make sense. It seems like the kind of mystery where you really need your wits about you. I hope we can leave tomorrow. We haven't been able to reach Worthington yet, so we have no idea what his schedule is and whether he can drive us, but I did manage to talk to Miss Bennett at the library and Pete should be getting here soon — "

"Pete's at the library?" Mallory interrupted.

"He's finishing that history paper he bailed on. Remember? After he hurt his wrist in softball at the end of the year and couldn't write or type. Anyway, there's one more thing I think will interest you," Bob said.

"I'm already interested," Mallory said, "but go on." After listening for a while she said, "Wow! A cathedral *and* a labyrinth. It's pretty intriguing – and it may be significant – that the poems were abandoned near an exact copy of the work of art that inspired them in the first place."

"I agree," Jupiter said. "But the heart of it is that Adam Suleiman wants us to try to figure out what was stolen from the portfolio the poems were in – and, if possible, get it back."

Mallory couldn't remember Jupiter ever being this excited at the beginning of a case. Usually it took some time for him to reach full speed. But the challenge of figuring out what was going on with so little information had turbocharged him, and it seemed to Mallory that, if he could have, Jupiter would have blasted off into space that minute for Alameda, with Bob, Mallory, and Pete trailing behind him.

Still, after Mallory had a full picture of everything that Bob and Jupiter knew – not all that much, but including the whole story involving the priest and the Suleiman family – Jupiter looked like he'd run out of gas.

"Why don't we go and sit in the outdoor workshop," he asked, "and wait for Pete to show up? He can't be much longer now."

As they were walking toward the workshop, the wooden gate at the back of the Salvage Yard swung open and Aunt Mathilda popped through. She was headed for the Office, but she stopped when she saw the three of them.

"Mallory!" she called. "At last! Time's a wasting! I'm hoping you can get some sorting done in the furniture shed. It's getting overcrowded again, and you know how happy I was with the order you managed to make out of all this mess."

Mallory felt a pang of guilt. She knew how much Aunt Mathilda depended on her.

"I promise I'll get to it just as soon as I can," she said, "but Jupiter and Bob have been telling me about a new case. It looks like we'll be heading up toward San Francisco for a little while. Starting tomorrow."

She almost winced, expecting Aunt Mathilda's response.

"Goodness gracious!" Aunt Mathilda said. "I can't keep track of the four of you any more. It seems you're almost never here. I'd almost say I'd started to miss you! How am I going to keep the Salvage Yard running?"

"We'll be back soon," Jupiter said, "and if Mallory can't get the work done by herself, we'll all pitch in."

Aunt Mathilda shook her head in mock dismay. "Go if you must. You know how proud I am of the four of you. Where did you say you were headed?'

"The Bay Area," Jupiter said. "Alameda and environs."

"Well, be careful," she said. "San Francisco has gotten very dangerous and dirty in recent years!"

"I know," Jupiter said – and to Mallory's surprise, his tone was very somber.

When they got to the workshop, they all sat down heavily as if they'd walked a great distance. Mallory had to admit that even a brief encounter with Aunt Mathilda could really take it out of you.

"I think we can do this," Jupiter said, "though we'll have to work fast in order to leave tomorrow. If Worthington can't take us, the priest, Father Samuel, has offered to drive us up in the van that belongs to his retirement home. What we need to do now is find a place to stay. Bob and I have been looking, but there are so many places to stay in the Bay area that we have no idea where to start – especially because we don't want to spend a lot of money on food."

"What does food have to do it?" asked Mallory.

"Jupiter means that it would be good if we could find a motel with some sort of little kitchen, but even though I'd have thought the area would be full of motels like that, it really isn't," Bob explained.

"The Tri-Faith Center, where the poems are headed, is in Oakland," Jupiter said, "but that's quite dangerous, too, these days. The Cathedral is in northern San Francisco, and the Suleimans live in Alameda, so ideally, we should stay somewhere close to all three places. But we should definitely stay somewhere *not* in the city."

Once again, Mallory was surprised by just how serious Jupiter sounded. Of course, no doubt San Francisco *was* a dangerous place these days, but just this summer The Three Investigators had run into pretty bad trouble not just once and not just twice but on four separate occasions, and Mallory had never heard Jupiter sound the way he sounded now. Clearly, it would improve his mood if she could find them a safe place to stay while they were there, so she opened her laptop and began searching.

Soon, she was feeling just as dismayed and discouraged as Bob had been by all the not-very-appealing choices. Most places were astronomically expensive or in neighborhoods that looked dicey. The more Mallory searched the more discouraged she felt, and all of a sudden she found herself saying, "What kind of country doesn't have decent hostels? The U.K. – and Scotland especially – is packed with them."

"What are hostels?" Bob asked. "I've heard of them, but I don't think I've ever seen one."

"They're for students, mostly," Mallory said. "They're cheap and clean and safe, and if you need to stay near a city in the U.K. – or just about anywhere else in Europe – and you're young, that's where you're going to want to go."

She typed "define hostel" into the search bar, and soon was reading aloud:

"'A supervised, inexpensive lodging place for travelers, especially young travelers. Generally, the rooms are like dormitories, with lots of beds or bunk beds. Sometimes they have meals or planned activities.'

"Anyway," she continued, "maybe we should ask Father Samuel if he knows of someplace cheap and safe, with kitchens, where we could stay."

However, Bob had opened his own laptop and he surprised Mallory by saying, "There's a place called the Golden Gate Hostel on the other side of the Golden Gate Bridge. It's in Marin County, and it looks like it would be pretty close to both Grace Cathedral and The Tri-Faith Center – and not all that far from Alameda. Do you want me to send you the link?"

"That's all right," said Mallory. "I'll look it up myself." Soon she was staring at a photograph of a large Victorian building that had apparently once been a military hospital but now looked more like an inn.

"Good Lord," said Mallory. "This really *is* a hostel! And a nice one. With a communal kitchen and free Wi-Fi. And look at this! They have an open bedroom starting tomorrow. And it's got four beds! It's like it's been waiting for us to arrive!"

"Book it!" Jupiter said. "Waste no time."

Mallory tried to follow his instructions, but for some reason the reservation arm of the hostel's website was having a slow day. As she waited for one thing and another to happen, she had plenty of time to realize that if she *did* manage to book this room, it would be the first time she'd ever stayed with the boys alone in the same room overnight.

Of course, on their last case, all four of them *had* stayed in the same attic at Connor O'Malley's house, but Califia García-Williams and Branko Petrovic had been with them at the time, and Mallory and Califia had put their sleeping bags next to one another and at some distance from the boys. So this would really be something new.

Mallory felt a little funny about that right now, but if she was going to remain The Three Investigators' Special Consultant, this sort of sleeping arrangement would have to happen sometime, and when the hostel's website suddenly started working again, it looked as if *now* was going to be that sometime.

The reservation secured, Mallory went back to the slideshow photographs the hostel has posted in order to let Bob and Jupiter see them. The kitchen was large and light-filled, with what looked like a professional range. The public rooms were filled with Victorian architectural touches. There were long views of the Golden Gate Bridge and the Pacific Ocean.

"Can you see that stuff from the hostel itself?" Bob asked. He looked gobsmacked.

"I don't know," Mallory said. "We'll have to wait and see." She, too, was now quite excited about the trip and the case. After all, for all intents and purposes, she was finished with her plans for HQ2, and it really *would* be great to solve one final mystery before the school year began. If it worked out the way they hoped it would, they'd really have something to celebrate when they got back to Rocky Beach. In the meantime, it would be good if she learned a little more about the case.

She turned to Bob. "You said the stolen poems were inspired by a labyrinth in the floor of the Chartres Cathedral?" she asked

"Yes," Bob said. "Apparently they're about the pilgrim's journey toward God – which the labyrinth symbolizes."

"And there's an exact copy of the labyrinth in the cathedral in San Francisco?" Mallory asked.

"Yes," Jupiter said. "You should look it up."

In no time, she was staring at images of the labyrinth in the floor of Grace Cathedral. It was stunning, she thought – intricate and simple at the same time, a beautiful design that gave the impression of symmetry but was actually asymmetrical.

"And you said the poems were all villanelles?" she asked.

"Yes," said Bob. "Though I'm not sure what a villanelle even is. We haven't had time to look it up yet. Do you know?"

"I think I might," Mallory said. "In Scotland, I had a seventh-grade English teacher who taught my class a section called Great Poets of the United Kingdom, and we studied a Welsh poet named Dylan Thomas. I think one of his poems was a villanelle."

"So look it up," said Bob.

She did – and when she saw it, she wished she hadn't. The poem was a plea to Dylan Thomas's dying father entitled "Do not go gentle into that good night," and when Mallory clicked on a link that led her to it, tears filled her eyes. The last time she'd read it, her own father had been hale and hearty, but he had died less than a year afterwards – and although the circumstances had been very different, the poem spoke deeply to her, anyway.

Still, she didn't want Bob and Jupiter to see that she was crying, so she pretended a bug had landed on her face and managed to wipe the tears off before anyone saw them. Then she went to a Wikipedia article about villanelles, and in a cool, calm, and collected voice – at least she hoped so! – she read that the form was originally French. Just as was true in the Dylan Thomas poem, all villanelles were supposed to have nineteen rhyming lines – five stanzas of three lines each and a final stanza of four lines. The first and third lines of the first stanza were repeated throughout the poem – verbatim.

She handed her laptop to Bob so he could see the repetition and rhyme scheme in chart form.

"Boy," Bob said, as he studied it. "It looks as if that would be pretty hard. Not just to mimic it, but to make it into a decent poem."

"I agree," Mallory said. "You'd need to make a very particular repetition work, without having it become boring. But there's something restful about reading formal poetry – and writing it must be a little like designing a building."

"What do you mean?" Bob asked.

"Oh, I don't know," Mallory said. "It was just a thought."

"An interesting thought," said Jupiter, taking Mallory's laptop away from Bob and studying the rhyme scheme himself. "In the

same way that a timber-frame structure fits together using age-old techniques, a poem like
this one could be said to have its own sort of
mortise and tenon fittings.”

“That’s exactly right,” Mallory said.
“Formal poems are like the − I don’t know −
the lexical equivalent of a building that uses a
lot of traditional techniques and forms, but uses
them in a new way.”

Mallory didn’t think she’d ever used the
word “lexical” aloud in a sentence before but
she really liked the way it sounded.

Just then, Pete arrived on his bicycle,
and by the time Mallory, Bob, and Jupiter had
managed to give him a bare bones explanation
as to what was up, it was also time for Mallory
to try to get a little work done in the Salvage
Yard so that Aunt Mathilda didn’t blow a gas-
ket.

Leaving Bob and Jupiter to explain a villanelle to a befuddled-looking Pete, Mallory
made her way to her favorite work shed. But
instead of starting work, she found herself looking around, still thinking about words and poems and buildings. And then Mallory thought
about Adam Suleiman and his father Jacob.

Jacob Suleiman was an architect. He designed buildings. Maybe when they got to

Alameda, Mallory could show him her design for HQ2 and get his input and advice. That wouldn't be why they were there, of course, and if Jupiter had his way, the subject would never even come up.

Even so, Mallory liked and admired Jupiter more and more with every passing case, and while she knew that the challenge of figuring out what had been stolen from a secret pocket in an ancient leather portfolio of poems – not to mention *who* had stolen it, and why – would defeat most human beings, she had a funny feeling it wouldn't defeat *him*.

4

Pirate Treasure

The next morning, as he packed for the trip to San Francisco, Pete was feeling a little torn about leaving Rocky Beach again so soon – especially because, this time, Califia García-Williams wouldn't be going with them. At least he'd talked to her on the phone that morning, and he grinned as he remembered her telling him to take care of himself up in what she'd called "crazytown."

Worthington was going to be busy for the next three days – driving for a small group taking a wine tour of the Temecula Valley – and he couldn't take them up to the Bay area, so the priest, Father Samuel, who Pete hadn't met yet, would be picking them up later this morning. Pete's mother would be driving him to the Salvage Yard once he had his gear assembled.

According to Jupiter – who'd called to tell him the plans – Father Samuel would be staying at a home for retired priests run by the San Franciscan diocese, and he'd been given permission to take the van he'd been driving when Jupiter had met him.

When Pete had asked about bringing their bikes, Jupiter had said no. Too dangerous, and too slow. They'd probably have to take taxis or a car-service, he said.

As Pete finished packing, he noticed the draft of the history paper he'd been working on lying on his desk and wondered if he should take it with him. Although he wasn't usually all that excited about assigned papers, this time he'd picked a great topic. He was writing about Lieutenant Stephen Decatur, one of the first naval heroes of what then had been the brand-new United States of America. When one of the first American warships – a ship called the *Philadelphia* – had been captured by pirates in the Mediterranean, Decatur had reclaimed the ship, then burned it to the waterline.

Pete had been amazed to learn that, in the old days, there was a place in North Africa called the Barbary Coast, and its ports were home to bands of pirates known as corsairs. When ships sailed through the Straits of Gibraltar, the narrow entrance to the Mediterranean Sea, corsairs would board and seize them, ransack the cargo, and demand ransom from the country from which the ship had sailed if it wanted its ship back.

Corsairs from a place called Tripoli had captured the *Philadelphia* not all that long after the American Revolution was over, Pete now knew. Even more amazing was the fact that the Barbary pirates usually sold the crew and whoever else was on board as slaves. Over a million Europeans had been sold into slavery between 1700 and 1900. This had really surprised Pete. Up until then, he had thought that all slaves had come from Africa. But he'd read that the Europeans had been sold *as* slaves in northern Africa – and also in southeastern Europe and western Asia.

He picked up his paper-in-progress, then put it down, then picked it up again. It was only half-finished, but he knew how it was going to end. Between 1784 and 1793, twelve ships from the brand-new United States of America had been taken by the pirates. That was why Congress had created the United States Navy in 1794 – because Thomas Jefferson had wanted this ransom business to stop.

Pete stuffed his unfinished paper into his backpack, tossed his sleeping bag over his shoulder, and ran downstairs to where his mother was waiting. On the way to the Salvage Yard, Pete told her a bit about Father Samuel, and for a moment she seemed quite interested.

"You went to Catholic school, didn't you?" Pete asked.

"I certainly did," his mother said. "But I was taught by nuns, not priests wearing cassocks!"

She herself was wearing her big hoop earrings today and they flashed in the sun. She didn't look like a Catholic girl. She looked like a gypsy, Pete thought.

"But let's not talk about that," she said. "Why don't you tell me about your rafting trip and your last adventure? You've said very little about it, Pete."

"I know," Pete said. "But we just got back."

"It's almost like you have a little secret," his mother said. She glanced at him and the expression on her face was hard to read.

Pete tensed. Uh oh, he thought. Sometimes it seemed she could almost read his mind. What his mother really wanted to talk about was Califia García-Williams.

How had she guessed that his feelings toward Califia had deepened? It wasn't that he didn't want his mother to know about Califia, but the whole thing seemed so new. It was too soon to talk about it. He'd thought she was doing him a favor by driving him to the Salvage Yard, but really she'd just wanted to trap him in the car so she could interrogate him!

"The trip was great!" Pete said brightly, glancing out the window at the passing houses. "Look! The Browns are painting their house!."

"Did anything interesting happen?" his mother asked. She'd turned the air conditioner on and the noise of the blowing air made her a little hard to hear.

"Interesting?" Pete asked. "Other than having Branko and Califia get kidnapped by a brain-damaged man who was being controlled by a maniac?"

"How *is* Califia?" his mother asked, zeroing in, her voice calm and smooth. "I hope she wasn't too upset."

Bingo! Pete thought. "No," he said. He thought of how brave Califia had been and he found himself smiling. "She took it in stride. She's – she's – "

"But then she is the most remarkable girl, isn't she?" his mother said. "So talented."

"She really is," Pete said, warming to the topic. "She was supposed to pretend she was channeling Odetta Dharmapuki singing, and you should have heard her."

"I wish I had," her mother said. "Maybe

you could invite her over to the house some time."

"What?" Pete said, turning to look at her. "So you can hear her sing?"

This was hopeless! She was so good at this!

His mother frowned. "What's the matter with you?" she said. "You're not usually this – this – "

"This what?" Pete asked. "Maybe I just don't want to talk about her."

"Don't you like her?" his mother asked innocently. Pete knew she already knew the answer. She was just trying to get him to admit it. He'd attempted to be as noncommittal as possible, but she kept asking the wrong questions. Or maybe the right questions – as far as getting him to talk went.

"Of course I like her!" he said – perhaps a little too loudly.

His mother looked at him, a big smile on her face. It reminded him of times when he'd been younger and had done something wrong and how she'd always gotten him to confess.

"You're almost fifteen," she said. "That's not too young to be thinking about a girlfriend."

"Mom!" Pete yelled. Now she'd made

him blush, and it was a bad one. He felt the heat rising up his neck, his cheeks, his scalp. He knew if he could see his face right now he'd look like a boiled lobster.

"I just wanted you to know you can talk to me," his mother said, solicitously. "About anything. Anything at all."

"I know," Pete said. "Thanks." But at the moment he didn't feel very grateful. In fact, he thought he'd never been so glad to see the wrought-iron gates of the Salvage Yard appear. "We're here!" he said.

"And just think," his mother said. "Tonight you'll be sleeping in a hostel north of San Francisco."

"I know," Pete said.

"Too bad Califia won't be with you," she said.

"But Mallory will be," Pete said. There. That should give her something to think about!

"But – " his mother said.

"Thanks, Mom," Pete said, reaching across the seat to give her a quick hug and a kiss. "See you in a few days."

"Be careful," she said, "and have fun." That was what she always said.

As she drove away, Pete felt just a touch of triumph. He dropped his gear on the front steps of the Salvage Yard's office and went off to find Mallory, Bob, and Jupiter. They had to be in Headquarters.

They were all sitting looking at the new computer display Zachary Hughes had given The Three Investigators as a thank-you present, along with the computer attached to it.

Someone had gotten up a map of their route from Rocky Beach to the hostel where they'd be staying, and Jupiter had tagged the locations of three of the places they'd need to get to from the hostel. Although Pete had never been a great fan of computers – and wasn't all that fond of maps, either – he was amazed at how crisp and clear the high-resolution cinema display was.

"There's Oakland," Mallory said, pointing, "and there's Sausalito."

Pete followed closely as Bob traced their route – up Interstate 5 to where they turned west on Interstate 580 and then up to Oakland where they joined Interstate 80 and crossed the Oakland Bay Bridge. From the times he'd been in the city before, he remembered how long the bridge was, and how crowded it was with traffic. He'd almost stopped paying attention when Bob said, "Wow! Look at that! I never noticed that before. An island in the Bay is called Treasure Island."

"Treasure Island?" Pete said. "You mean, like the book with the pirates? I've been writing about pirates!"

"I was meaning to ask you," Bob said. "How's the paper coming?"

"Almost finished," Pete said. "And if I ever complain about having to write another one, remind me how much cool stuff you can learn. Before I started, I didn't even know there *were* pirates in the Mediterranean."

"Is that what you're writing about?" asked Mallory.

"Yes, but not exactly," Pete said. "There were two whole wars called the Barbary Wars that the U.S. Navy fought with the pirates. My paper's about one of the country's very first naval heroes. His name was Lieutenant Stephen Decatur. During the First Barbary War, an American warship called the USS *Philadelphia* ran aground, and the Barbary pirates captured the ship and its crew and dragged them back to Tripoli.

"Decatur and sixty men put together a really risky mission to free the ship, but when he couldn't, he set it on fire so the enemy couldn't use it. Then he became Captain Stephen Decatur," Pete said triumphantly.

"Thomas Jefferson knew it was a lot more important to stop the pirates from taking any more ships than it was to get that one particular ship back."

"It's weird that you've been reading about the Barbary Wars when the Suleimans used to live in Morocco," Bob said. "Morocco was part of the Barbary Coast."

"It *was?*" Pete said. But before anyone had the chance to answer, the intercom between Headquarters and the office squawked and Aunt Mathilda's voice said, "The priest is here!"

They found Father Samuel on the front steps of the office, trying to talk to Aunt Mathilda, who looked happy to see the four of them arrive. After Jupiter had introduced Pete, Mallory, and Bob to Father Samuel, Pete and Jupiter loaded their gear into the back of the van while Mallory and Bob chatted with the priest.

"Goodbye," Aunt Mathilda said as the van backed up and began to turn around. "Good luck, and be sure to remember what I said about San Francisco, and how dirty and dangerous and – "

Pete strained to hear her last words, but the van's noises drowned them out. He found himself in the front seat with Father Samuel.

Mallory and Jupiter sat in the second row of seats, and Bob had the third row all to himself.

It was awkward in the beginning. No one seemed to know what to say, and the priest seemed to be what Pete's mother would have called "concentrating on his driving." But as they left Rocky Beach and headed east toward Interstate 5, things became a bit more relaxed.

"This is really quite exciting for me," Father Samuel said. "Since I retired, I spend most of my days walking or thinking or reading by myself. It's a treat to be with four interesting young people – especially ones who come so highly recommended by Adam Suleiman."

"That's very kind of you," Jupiter said, from behind the priest. "I hope we live up to Adam's expectations."

"Oh, I'm sure you will," Father Samuel said. "Now tell me. What have you been up to this morning?"

At first no one said anything, and then, embarrassed by the silence, Pete jumped in.

"We were looking at maps of the trip," he said, "and I was telling them about pirates."

"Pete's writing a paper about one of the country's very first naval heroes," Jupiter said. "It's hard to remember, given how strong the military is now, but after the Revolution, the country was actually small and weak. The Barbary pirates took advantage of that."

"The Barbary pirates," the priest said nostalgically, as though they were friends of his. "That reminds me. I don't think I ever told Mr. Jones the history of the portfolio that was stolen and then returned."

"Who's Mr. Jones?" Pete asked.

Jupiter laughed. "That would be me, I think," he said.

"You can call him Jupiter," Pete said. "I do."

"All right," the priest said, smiling. "Anyway, my story is a long and complicated one and takes shape over several hundred years."

Oh no, Pete thought. He snuck a glance back at Jupiter who looked slightly alarmed. He had told Pete and the others about how the priest had a roundabout way of telling a story.

Pete took it upon himself to keep the old man on track. "My mother told me," he said, "to start at the beginning and then to just keep going."

"Very wise advice," the priest said, "though I've come to believe it is somewhat difficult to know where the beginning is. Do I start with the building of the cathedral itself?

Or with the creation of the labyrinth? With what was happening in France in the Middle Ages?"

This was going to be harder than Pete had thought.

"Why don't you start as close to the present as you possibly can?" he asked.

"I'll start with the writing of the poems themselves," the priest said.

"The twelve villanelles," Mallory said, helpfully, from the second row. Pete looked back to see Jupiter's resigned expression and stifled a snort.

"Yes indeed," the priest said. "Of course Jacques de Boissy was already a Catholic when he visited the cathedral at Chartre, but from what I've been able to gather, not a particularly *committed* Catholic."

"What does that mean?" Pete asked.

The priest looked embarrassed. "Let's just say he didn't follow all of the Church's teachings," he said. "But when he started writing the poems, he felt as though he'd been possessed by God — as if God were dictating the poems to him. The experience was so spiritual, so ethereal, that de Boissy became a fervent Catholic."

"That's really interesting," Bob said.

It actually was, Pete thought.

The priest went on. "The experience was so personal, so intimate, that de Boissy refrained from showing the poems to anyone outside his family. He thought it would be unseemly, even crass, to capitalize on them. After all, they had been dictated to him by God! So they remained unpublished and were passed down through the generations for almost a hundred and fifty years."

"What happened then?" Pete asked.

There was a long pause as the van trundled along the highway, but this time Pete decided to keep his mouth shut and just let Father Samuel continue in his own good time.

Soon he did.

"In the early 1700s, de Boissy's descendants commissioned the well-known English poet Wilfred Willoughby to do a translation," he said. "They needed a real poet to do the job, because they needed someone who could do more than just translate words from one language to another. They needed someone who would be able to write a convincing and eloquent villanelle."

He sighed, as he thought about this.

"After that, the poems were finally published – in both French and English. Eventually they came to the attention of Pope Benedict XIV, who asked to see the originals – the ones that de Boissy had written out by hand."

"Why did he want to see those?" Bob asked from the back seat. "Couldn't he just have read the printed versions?"

Father Samuel nodded. "Yes, of course," he said. "But God works in mysterious ways, and by then the world knew about de Boissy's belief that the poems had been dictated. Perhaps His Holiness wanted to see the handwriting that had come directly from the mouth of God. So the family – they lived in Bordeaux, where they had made a great deal of money from their vineyard – put the poems in a leather-bound portfolio they had specially made. Then they put it on a ship from Bordeaux to Italy, together with a shipment of French wine. This would have been in the late 1700s."

Pete was beginning to get a feeling that he knew where this story was headed. He could hardly believe it.

"The French ship sailed through the Straits of Gibraltar and on into the Mediterranean – "

"Where it was seized by Barbary pirates!" Pete exclaimed.

The priest looked at him mildly. "Yes, indeed, my son. I'm surprised you would guess
that. Oh, yes, of course. You're writing a paper about them. The wonders of American
education. I went, of course, to Catholic
schools, but one of the priests – "

"You were saying the ship sailed into the
Mediterranean?" Pete said, before the priest
could get deflected.

"Yes," Father Samuel said. "So, as you
noted, the pirates seized the ship, took all the
wine and the other goods, and also the portfolio of poems."

"And they probably sold the crew as
slaves," Pete said.

"That is possible," the priest said. "I do
not know. But back in France, when the news
reached them, the family was distraught. They
thought the original handwritten poems were
lost forever, but it seems that some of those pirates were better educated than you would
have expected, and eventually the portfolio
made its way to Casablanca, in Morocco,
where they were obtained by a Christian family
that kept them in their private library."

What a great story! Pete had thought
the old man would never get around to the
main point, but he had, and now Pete was glad

he had taken his time. It made the story better.

"So how did it wind up with the Suleimans?" he asked the priest.

"But I thought you understood," the priest said. "The Suleimans *were* the Christian family from Casablanca that came into possession of the portfolio," the priest said.

"The Suleimans!" Pete said. "Wow! So they've owned the poems since the 17th century?"

"Yes," the priest said. "For over three hundred and fifty years."

This was amazing! Pete thought. The very family – or at least a small part of it – that they were going to visit the next day! And the portfolio, which had been returned to them with the poems in it, and which he and the others were going to see – were going to hold in their hands – had been in the hands of Barbary pirates! Maybe even the ones who had captured the USS *Philadelphia* and then had had it burned from underneath them by Stephen Decatur.

While that would certainly be a big coincidence, it wasn't impossible. Or maybe it was.

The thing was, although Bob and Jupiter and Mallory were all pretty interested in history and had a good grasp of what happened when and where in the past of the human species, Pete had always been more interested in the here and now. But although he was really looking forward to meeting this guy Adam, and hearing from his own lips exactly why he had been so certain The Three Investigators were the right people to help him and his father figure out what had gone missing from their portfolio, he wasn't all that excited about going to San Francisco.

It wasn't that he was apprehensive about of the city, exactly, but it was a whole lot different from the Napa Valley and Santa Barbara and Rocky Beach and Jackson and Auburn – which were the other places The Three Investigators had conducted investigations this summer. Still, whatever might happen, as long as the four of them were together, they'd be able to deal with it, Pete thought – or, rather, hoped!

5

Into The Labyrinth

By the time the van with Father Samuel at the wheel had turned west, off Interstate 5 and onto Interstate 580, Jupiter was feeling a little tired. It had been seven hours since they'd left Rocky Beach – most of them in the van, though they'd stopped for lunch along the way and had treated Father Samuel, who had been almost too grateful.

The priest was a kind and well-meaning man, Jupiter thought, but he had certain habits of mind that made him a somewhat tiresome companion. He seemed unable to get to the point of any story he was telling. He was forever circling back to include some unnecessary detail. And he clearly liked to talk. All the way up in the van, he had assailed them with anecdotes from his entire career as a priest.

Jupiter looked forward to their arrival at the Golden Gate Hostel where he could have some uninterrupted thinking time. Even so, he'd tried as best he could to shut out the conversation in the van and to focus on the part of Father Samuel's story that interested him most.

Someone had taken something from a secret pocket in the leather portfolio. But who that was, and what had been taken – those were mysteries that needed to be solved.

Perhaps, Jupiter thought, he could use the few details the priest had just given them in order to figure out who had known about the secret pocket to begin with. After all, it was a perfect test of the kind of critical thinking he was trying to describe to Harper in his letter – and also something he enjoyed a lot.

The first person Jupiter thought of was the one who had actually made the portfolio – most probably a French leatherworker. Had he made the secret pocket on a whim? Or because he'd been asked to by de Boissy's family, as part of his commission? One way or another, the artisan would have known about the hiding place in the portfolio he himself had made.

Whoever had packed the twelve poems up for the Pope would also have known – if indeed he or she had put into the secret pocket whatever had now been taken out of it.

"We're getting close to Oakland," Pete said. Pete was always on the lookout for landmarks and unusual sights and liked to point them out.

"Yes," Bob said. "It won't be long now."

"These Interstates are awful," Mallory said. "How can people stand them?"

"I'm quite pleased that the traffic is not too bad," the priest said, then began telling a story about a traffic jam he'd once gotten stuck in. Jupiter went back to thinking.

It could have been a single member of de Boissy's family, Jupiter thought, or the whole family could have known. Or perhaps even someone who wasn't a member of the family but who had somehow gotten their hands on the portfolio and was hijacking it for their own purposes.

But who could that be? Jupiter wondered. Someone who wanted to send something in secret to the Pope? Probably not the leatherworker, but someone who knew what the portfolio was to be used for and who'd persuaded him to create the secret pocket so that he – the unknown person – could use it? Under that scenario, the secret item would have already been hidden in the secret pocket when the portfolio was delivered to de Boissy's family.

There was only one problem with this train of thought. How would the Pope have known that there was a secret pocket to begin with and that he should go looking for whatever was in it?

Anyway, Jupiter was pleased to have narrowed down the suspects to two people or two sets of people – whoever had used the secret pocket was either a member of the family that had sent the portfolio off, or the leatherworker or someone close to him. They were the ones who could have put something in. But who had taken that something out? And maybe even more important, what *was* that something?

There was no way of knowing, but Jupiter could speculate. A map, perhaps, leading to some hidden treasure? A military or religious document of some kind?

Maybe the mystery item wasn't being sent to the Pope himself but to someone at the Vatican who planned to intercept the portfolio and remove the item before delivering the poems to the Pope. Jupiter groaned. Maybe he was making this harder than it needed to be.

He looked up to see that they were approaching the Bay Bridge and his mind moved away from his questions about the case as he stared at this astonishing feat of engineering. He had seen it before, but it was still amazing.

It was four-and-a-half miles long, connecting Oakland and San Francisco across the San Francisco Bay. It was divided into two almost equal sections, the eastern and western, which met on Yerba Buena Island in the middle of the Bay. Jupiter had read that it carried upwards of a quarter million cars a day.

All of them were now intently studying the bridge as they came to the toll plaza in Oakland and then began the crossing. To the north, the skyscrapers of San Francisco's Financial District clustered together and got larger the closer they came to them. Though it was not yet dusk, the lights had come on and the glass and steel rectangles glittered. It was an impressive sight.

"Once we get into the city," Bob said, "we turn north and head straight for Nob Hill. It's amazing how close we'll come to Grace Cathedral."

"Maybe we should stop and see it on the way to the hostel," Jupiter said. Since he hadn't expected to say this (or to think it), this surprised him, but since Grace Cathedral had been where the portfolio had surfaced after it was stolen, he had a sudden urge to inspect the place for himself as soon as possible.

Though he had no idea what he expected to discover, he thought perhaps he could talk with whoever ran the Lost and Found – who might conceivably know which pew it had been left in. It would also be interesting to see the labyrinth – just like the one that had inspired the poems.

Jupiter leaned forward in his seat to bring him closer to the priest.

"Father Samuel, would it be all right with you if we stopped at the cathedral?" he said.

"I wouldn't mind at all," Father Samuel said. "You'll have to go in without me, so that I can stay and guard the van. I can't let some lunatic smash the windows or slash the tires! But I've already been inside the cathedral three or four times myself. It's a lovely place, French Gothic in style, with a stunning rose window. And, of course, the labyrinth! It's Episcopalian but still very much like the old Catholic cathedrals in Europe. And its message today is very ecumenical, very welcoming. But the Episcopal Church was not always like that."

To Jupiter, it seemed that the sigh that accompanied this remark was of a very long-drawn-out nature.

"What do you mean?" Pete asked.

"You probably never studied English history," said Father Samuel. "But when King Henry VIII wanted his first marriage annulled so he could marry again, he petitioned the

Pope – who refused him. Henry broke away from the Catholic Church and founded the Church of England – the Episcopal Church – with himself as its Supreme Head."

Here, Father Samuel sighed again, even more emphatically than the first time.

"The break had to be complete," he went on, "so Henry and his allies and the kings that followed him did everything they could to wipe out the Catholic Church in England. They dissolved monasteries and convents; they toppled religious statues; they imprisoned and executed Catholics and destroyed artifacts and paintings and monuments and buildings."

As Jupiter listened, he realized Father Samuel had been right; neither he nor Bob and Pete had ever studied this history. Maybe Mallory had, being from Scotland, but this was new information to him.

"They felt that in order to get English Catholics to become members of the new Church, they had to demolish all signs of everything that had come before," Father Samuel continued. "It affected a lot of Catholics – even outside of England – very badly. People lost their faith in God."

"Just like Adam's father," said Pete.

"Yes," said Father Samuel. "Just like Jacob. I don't know what I'd do without God in my life. I'd be completely lost. I feel the same way about knowledge of the past. Thomas Aquinas studied Socrates and wrote that 'the memory of past things is necessary for us to deliberate well about future things'."

"Who was Thomas Aquinas?" Pete asked.

"An Italian saint," said Father Samuel. "But a big believer in reason. Both a philosopher and a theologian."

Though Jupiter had heard of Thomas Aquinas, he didn't know much about him, so he was surprised to hear that a medieval theologian had also been a rationalist. Perhaps his own view of religion was too narrow, Jupiter thought. Not only had some of the greatest achievements of the human species been undertaken to honor God, or gods, but perhaps the best theologians had always been philosophers.

And then the van was in downtown San Francisco, tall buildings all around them. Father Samuel didn't seem bothered to be driving in urban traffic, and he also seemed to know his way around the city. Jupiter had to give him a lot of credit. Somehow he found Highway 101 – which here was called Van Ness Avenue – and then turned right for a couple of blocks before pulling up close to Grace Cathedral on California Street.

"An oasis in the desert," Father Samuel said, looking at the cathedral's facade. "This city has fallen on hard times. These days it seems a hot-bed of chaos," he added as he parked.

"Bob was just saying that people seem to like to make chaos out of order," Jupiter said, nodding. And then he found himself adding, "Our first case this summer involved a fake monk in a Franciscan monastery in the Napa Valley. His name was Brother Anders Bergmann. He was born in San Francisco, and when I asked him about his favorite part of the city, he said something about the whole city being a mix of order and chaos."

As soon as he'd said this, Jupiter wished he could take it back. After all, a priest like Father Samuel wasn't likely to want to hear about fake monks!

As they got out of the van, Father Samuel told them again that he'd stay with it while the four of them went in. Jupiter looked up at the cathedral's two tall rectangular bell towers flanking the high arched entrance over which shone the large rose window. He thought the cathedral very striking.

Inside, it was dim and cool, and Jupiter's eyes flew up, past the slender, seemingly delicate stone piers, to the vaulted roof and its array of lights. Both sides of the cathedral were lined with ranked tall stained-glass windows topped with a smaller rose window that echoed the enormous window on the cathedral's façade.

But Jupiter was most taken with the labyrinth. Inlaid in the stone floor, it was massive, taking up the entire width of the nave. It looked exactly like the photograph of the labyrinth in the Chartres cathedral, although the colors were different. Here the stone was a very pale gray, almost white, with much darker gray markings that created the intricate winding switchbacked route to the six-petaled rose at the center.

Seeing the labyrinth in person was truly inspiring, Jupiter thought. He looked up to see that he was not the only one so affected. Pete, Mallory, and Bob all stood at the edge of the labyrinth's outermost circle, staring with expressions of extreme concentration.

"I read that there are sometimes chairs covering it," Bob said, "for the church's congregation. So we're lucky it's been cleared today. I guess once a week people come in here for yoga classes."

"I think we should try walking it," Mallory said. "If we come again later, the chairs may be back."

"Are there any rules?" Pete asked.

"I don't think so," Bob said. "You just walk in, at your own pace, and then back out again, thinking whatever you want to think. Even if you don't believe in the traditional concept of God, you can find what you *do* have faith in and think your own thoughts."

"I'll go first," Pete said. He stood at the entrance and took a step in, as if waiting to see if something happened before moving on. When nothing did, he took a second step and then a third. Bob followed him, and Mallory followed Bob.

Jupiter went last, walking slowly, purposefully putting one foot down and then the next in the winding pathways of the labyrinth. Alternately he looked down at his feet and around him at his friends who were now spread out within the elaborate work of art. Surprisingly, as he walked, he found himself returning to what he had been thinking about earlier, wondering who had put something in the portfolio's secret pocket – the leatherworker or the family? – and what had been hidden there.

Pete had made it to the center quite quickly and was soon threading his way back out. He passed Jupiter without speaking, smiling as he went, the two friends turning their bodies so they didn't touch. Bob and Mallory passed him in a likewise fashion.

When Jupiter got to the center, he stood for a moment, gazing down the main aisle of the cathedral, which was perfectly aligned with the main altar and the six-petaled rose. It was amazing what deep spiritual pleasure human beings took in harmony and symmetry and alignment – in order, he thought. The labyrinth was working on him.

When he finally reached the entrance – now the exit – he found Pete, Mallory, and Bob waiting for him.

"That was great!" Pete said.

"We thought as long as we're here, we'd look at the stained-glass windows and the art and the sculpture," Mallory said.

"You can do that," Jupiter said. "I just want to walk around and think."

With his mind as clear as it had become, he didn't know where it would take him, but he wanted to be open to whatever happened. As he was wandering down the cathedral's center aisle, he noticed a woman with a bucket and mop and suddenly wondered if she might be the person who'd discovered the portfolio the day it had been abandoned on one of the cathedral's pews.

She looked at him questioningly as he approached, and it struck Jupiter as probable that not too many of the cathedral's visitors stopped to speak with her.

"Hello," he said. "This is the first time I've ever been here, and it's quite magnificent."

The woman nodded and seemed proud of the place where she worked. "I've been here for over fifteen years and it still takes my breath away every time," she said reverently.

"You do a wonderful job," Jupiter said. "The place is immaculate."

"Why thank you," the woman said, leaning on her mop. "Of course there are a bunch of us. I'm not the only one."

"I wonder if you'd heard about a leather portfolio that was found in one of the pews a few days ago," Jupiter said. "My friends and I were called in to help the family that owned it."

"Heard about it?" the woman said in amazement. "I'm the one who found it."

"Is that so?" Jupiter asked.

"Yes, indeed," the woman said. "I knew right away it was something very special – not just one of those things that gets left behind by accident, like a school notebook or an old scarf."

"Did you happen to open the portfolio?" Jupiter asked.

The woman looked embarrassed.

"No," she said. "It didn't seem like my place to do that, but when I brought it to Mr. Tobin – he runs the Lost and Found – he opened it, and he and the Dean both told me how important the poems were."

"Do you remember anything special or unusual about the day you found the portfolio?" Jupiter asked. "Any people you remember seeing who struck you as out of the ordinary, or who were in the area near the pew where you found the portfolio? Where was that, by the way?"

"This one," the woman said, gesturing to a dark wooden bench nearby. "It was right at the end, almost behind the stone column, almost out of sight."

Jupiter could see the shadow the stone pier threw across the seats and how the portfolio had been left in a protected place – protected both for the portfolio and for the person who had left it. He found that interesting.

Of course, the very fact that the portfolio had been left in the church at all suggested that whoever had left it here had wanted to make as certain as he or she could that it wouldn't be harmed or stolen. But as Jupiter looked at the stone column to which the woman was gesturing, he could see that whoever might sit beside it would be almost unseen by those ahead of and behind him.

"And yes," the woman said. "To answer your question, there *was* something unusual going on that day in the cathedral – a special ecumenical service, for all faiths. There were a lot of people who had never been here before – rabbis and imams and priests and lots of regular people, so no one stood out at all. They released a thousand white paper doves on a column of light. I was way over there – " she indicated a place on the far side of the nave and toward the front – "so I'd never have seen who was in that area, even if I'd been looking."

"Even so, thank you very much for your time," Jupiter said.

"I'm happy to help," the woman said as she went back to her mopping.

Jupiter walked carefully up and down the aisles for a little while longer, thinking about what he had just learned. Whoever had returned the portfolio had certainly chosen a good time to do it – a time when he or she would never have been noticed, and when the portfolio could have been left behind in the seat he or she was sitting in – and not long before the entire cathedral was cleared of worshippers.

Also, the white paper doves that hadn't been picked up and kept by the people at the service would have had to be cleared away after the worshippers left. Whoever had abandoned the portfolio must have known that a cleaning crew would be arriving soon. Perhaps he or she had even stood in the shadows, keeping an eagle eye fixed on the place where the portfolio lay, in order to make certain that when it was discovered, it was taken to the Lost and Found – as it had been. Only after making sure it was safe had he or she left the cathedral.

Jupiter looked around to see that Bob and Mallory were talking near the entrance to the labyrinth. Although Jupiter knew that Father Samuel was waiting for the four of them in the van, he suddenly had another thought that he wanted to pursue. Perhaps it had been no coincidence that the portfolio had been stolen just as the Suleimans were about to donate it to the Tri-Faith Center for the Study of the Abrahamic Religions. Perhaps whoever had taken it had read about the upcoming gift in the papers and had acted quickly.

He made a mental note to check all the newspaper coverage before they met with the Suleimans, then walked to rejoin Bob and Mallory.

"Where's Pete?" he asked them.

"He's talking to someone in the visitor center," Bob said. "Oh, no, he isn't. Here he is."

"Listen to this, guys," Pete said excitedly, loudly enough so that he might as well not have been whispering. "I've just been talking to someone who told me that there are actually three labyrinths in San Francisco. The cathedral has two – the one right here and one outside – and there's a different kind in Land's End Park, on the western side of the northern tip of the city."

"Really?" Mallory asked.

"The woman I talked to said we should be sure to go there," Pete continued. "I guess the area near it is like a sort of public stage, and it can get filled with street performers – musicians playing guitars and actors putting on little plays, and puppet shows and mimes."

Jupiter shook his head dubiously. "There may be a purpose to seeing that third labyrinth," he said, "but if it involves encountering mimes, maybe it's not really worth it."

"What don't you like about mimes?" Pete asked. He put his hands in front of him as though he were testing the limits of the invisible glass box he suddenly found himself in.

Jupiter laughed. "Exactly," he said. "In the meantime we should get going. We've left Father Samuel waiting a long time now, and we need to check into the hostel before it gets too late."

"Let's go then!" Mallory said. "I can hardly wait to see the place. It's neat that it used to be a military hospital."

Jupiter thought so, too. After all, when something changed its nature so radically, it was interesting on the face of it. Also, the pictures of the hostel seemed to promise a pleasant order, which he was looking forward to.

As they drove toward it, Jupiter really *did* see chaos all around him. There were people living in tents on the sidewalk, gigantic piles of trash in unexpected places, boarded-up storefronts and broken windows. Also lots of dazed-looking people wandering around, some pushing shopping carts, some half clothed.

What had happened to the place in recent years, Jupiter wondered? In San Francisco as it was today, it was actually pretty amazing that whoever had stolen the Suleiman portfolio had managed to leave it in Grace Cathedral without getting mugged on the way.

After traversing the light-bedecked Golden Gate Bridge as night began to fall – a mile-long crossing over dark ocean waters – Jupiter felt a lessening of tension, a feeling of relief as they entered Marin County. He'd felt even better when they stopped for dinner.

A little later – at Bob and Mallory's request – Father Samuel pulled up to Seong's Market, a small Korean grocery. The store was owned by an older Korean couple who were both there, working.

They nodded pleasantly to Jupiter and the others as they browsed the refrigerated cases and the wooden crates of fruits and vegetables – each with a colorful old-fashioned label with fancy script that said *California Bounty*. The prices were marked on the boxes in white chalk. Jupiter thought they were pretty high.

Bob and Mallory collected food for breakfast and lunch the next day and when they put everything down on the counter, Mrs. Seong came over to help.

"Good for you," she said brightly. "Too many young people eat junk food these days.

This is very nice, make a good meal. California produce is the best."

"Everything looks very fresh," Bob said agreeably, as he took out his wallet.

"Yes," Mrs. Seong said, nodding emphatically. "We just switch suppliers. This boy show up every other day. *California Bounty*. A big white truck with shelves inside. They carry everything! They drive right up, and my husband and me, we climb into the truck and choose what we want. A little more expensive, but very convenient and very good. They make a big success. Many trucks, and they bring all over, Oakland, Alameda. To all the farmers' markets, too, even up Walnut Creek and Danville and Concord. Big success."

Jupiter wasn't certain why Mrs. Seong was telling them all this, but he supposed she was happy to see calm, rational customers who were pleased to be on this side of the Golden Gate. As Bob and Mallory thanked her and picked up the bags she'd put the food in, she said, "You enjoy now!"

At least *someone* was making a big success of life in the Bay area these days. As Father Samuel, with Bob's help, finally pulled up in front of the Golden Gate Hostel, Jupiter was pleased to see it looked as calm and orderly and welcoming as it had looked on the Internet.

Father Samuel had talked non-stop ever since they'd left Seong's Market and now he wrapped up his remarks for the day by repeating what he'd said to Jupiter about God moving in mysterious ways. Jupiter had never been personally drawn to the idea of God, but since he'd started reading the book about human achievement through the ages, he'd found himself thinking that maybe religion had been more of a linchpin in the history of civilization than he had previously realized.

After all, some of the greatest achievements of the human species – great music and buildings, and works of literature, and voyages of exploration, and even inventions – had been undertaken to honor God, or gods. These works were a legacy for all of humankind – and anyone who wanted to be an architect or a composer or a philosopher, or even a writer, needed to study that legacy respectfully if they hoped to build on it in their lifetime.

Still, as the four of them gathered their luggage together, said goodbye to Father Samuel, and started walking toward the hostel, Jupiter found himself thinking that perhaps his encounter earlier that summer with Brother

Anders, that criminal-disguised-as-a-monk, had been bad for his perspective when it came to the matter of men of the cloth. Father Samuel could not be more of a naif, but for some absurd reason, when Jupiter had heard him say, for the second time since they'd met, that God worked in mysterious ways, he'd thought, for an instant, that the elderly priest might be trying to tell him something.

6

Disorder At Land's End

When Mallory awoke the next morning, she wasn't entirely sure where she was. Groggily, she watched sunlight stream through gauzy white curtains into a room that wasn't hers.

Though she was warm and comfortable, she was temporarily confused until she saw the sleeping forms of Jupiter, Bob, and Pete, each in his own separate wooden bunk – set around the edges of the room – and then she remembered that they were in the Golden Gate Hostel in Sausalito.

Mallory was on her back, her hands folded on her stomach, when she heard a muffled groan and looked over to see Bob propped up on his elbows, still half-asleep. His brownblond hair was disheveled and his face was splotchy.

When he saw her, he waved, and she waved back. Before long, Pete was awake too, yawning hugely and grunting as he tossed from side to side and then sat up. When he saw that Jupiter was still asleep, he put his finger to his lips, crept out of bed, and went over to look at

104

him.

Jupiter lay on his side, one arm stretched out over his head and the other hidden beneath the blanket. One of his feet stuck out. Pete grinned. He went to his bag and came back with a pencil, with which he proceeded to lightly touch Jupiter's foot. All of a sudden, Jupiter's eyes flew open.

"Pete," he said. "Even in my dream I knew it was you."

"Time to get up, Jupe," Pete said brightly. "You're just lucky there wasn't a bowl of warm water somewhere nearby. Come on. I'm starving."

It took longer than Mallory would have expected for the three boys to get showered and dressed and ready for breakfast. Although she was generally hardly even aware that Bob, Pete, and Jupiter *were* boys – as opposed to just friends and colleagues – there was definitely something about sleeping in the same room with them that brought home the differences between boys and girls.

When they'd all gotten into the room last room, Pete and Bob had engaged in the sort of roughhousing that boys frequently *did* engage in – but never in such close quarters to Mallory! And that business with the warm water –

well, girls not only wouldn't do that, they wouldn't even think of it.

She was ready very quickly, and she went into the hostel's living room. While she waited for the boys to join her, she looked at her plans for the new Three Investigators headquarters again.

She'd brought them with her, and she was hoping that, at some point, she'd be able to talk with Jacob Suleiman about them. In particular, she wanted to ask him how hard it would be to put a brand-new roof on an existing building.

After all, the shed she usually worked in really was the right size already, and the walls and foundation were very sturdy. But the roof was old and ugly, and she was really in love with her idea of a hip roof, a cathedral ceiling, a central cupola, and four long narrow dormers to let light in.

Even six weeks after it had happened, Mallory still thought it almost incredible that Jupiter had actually asked her to design a new headquarters when she knew how attached he was, even now, to the old one. He was really an amazing person – and the evening before, after they'd gotten to the hostel and before the roughhousing had started in the bunkroom, he and she had sat in the living room − right about where she was sitting now − and talked about the case.

She was always flattered when Jupiter asked her opinion about something, but somehow last night had been extra special. Before they had started talking privately, Jupiter had filled all three of them in on the thinking he'd done the day before about the portfolio and who might have known about the secret pocket. He'd also told them in detail about his conversation with the cleaning woman.

But it was only when Bob and Pete had gone back to the room that Jupiter had turned to Mallory and said, "I've been thinking about the personality and character of the person who left the portfolio in the cathedral, and I'm suddenly wondering if whoever it was might have been different from the person who took it.

After all, the thief might have a friend or partner or husband or wife who didn't approve of the theft and who wanted to make things right. Maybe the thief had no intention of returning the portfolio, but someone who knew him did so anyway. That would make what we're trying to unravel even harder."

Mallory thought for a minute. "If I'm

remembering this right," she said, "Occam's Razor suggests that the simplest explanation for something is often the best. The simplest explanation is that whoever took the portfolio wasn't after the poems at all but after whatever was hidden in the secret pocket. And when he got his hands on that, he had no use for the portfolio or the poems, so he abandoned them in a place where they'd be relatively safe until they were found and returned to the Suleimans."

"That would make him a pretty outstanding citizen," Jupiter said, "as well as unusually scrupulous for a criminal. I can imagine most thieves just trashing the portfolio after getting what they were after. Especially in San Francisco, the way it looks today. The thief took a chance by returning it."

"I agree," Mallory said. "As well as turning his back on a small fortune. But if even the Suleimans didn't know there was something hidden in the portfolio, how could you prove that anything had actually been taken? So, no theft, no real crime – or at least not one the police would be quick to investigate. Which is why we're here to begin with. Because we *will* investigate it."

However, Jupiter wasn't finished. "What

confounds me," he said, "is why the thief took whatever it was to begin with."

"And you can't deduce that because his motivation depends on what was taken," Mallory had answered.

"Yes," Jupiter said, nodding. "And we have to presume that whatever was taken was put in the portfolio three hundred and fifty years ago, either by someone in de Boissy's family, by the man who made the portfolio, or by someone who knew him."

"Maybe we could make a list of all the things that might have been in there," Mallory suggested. "After all, it wasn't a musical instrument. Or a cup of coffee. It has to have been a bunch of papers, right? I mean, nothing else would fit."

Jupiter sat back in his chair and pinched his bottom lip.

"Why don't we start with the idea that it was a secret message to the Pope," he said. He frowned. "But if that's what it was, why sew it up and hide it? The poems were going to the Pope, anyway. Why couldn't the letter go too? Whatever the letter might have said, it couldn't have been more worth saving than the poems, which were already two hundred years old."

"Maybe it wasn't a message but a secret

map of some kind," Mallory said.

"I thought of that, too," Jupiter said.

"But usually secret maps are treasure maps and why send a treasure map to the Pope?" Mallory asked. "Maybe it was a military map. Maybe the Pope asked the family – they were devout Catholics from everything we can gather – to send him information about what was going on in France at the time."

At that point, the two of them had both sat and thought for a moment

"Or maybe," Mallory had added, "it wasn't a map but just military information. Maybe a military document of some kind. Maybe it was hidden because whoever sent it knew about the threat of the Barbary pirates."

"That's possible," Jupiter said. "But if that's what it was, why would someone today need it or want it enough to steal the portfolio? It might have value as an historical document, and it might be of interest to a museum, but why would an individual risk stealing something like that? Thieves take things that will benefit them personally – usually something they want or something they can sell for hard cash."

"That's true," Mallory said. "And that's what makes this such a mystery. Those twelve poems – the only handwritten copies in existence – would seem likely to be more valuable than any military document."

"Unless it was a very special and unique document," Jupiter had said. "A political document like the Declaration of Independence or the Magna Carta would be more valuable, probably. I think political documents like that would trump art every single time."

They had left it at that the night before, but Mallory knew that since Father Samuel had told them he had to visit some old parishioners this morning – from the time he'd lived up here – and that he wouldn't be able to pick them up until early afternoon, Jupiter wanted Mallory and Bob to do some research this morning after breakfast.

At last, the boys were ready, and the four of them made their way to the communal kitchen – a large room with pale green cabinets and two huge commercial stoves. They'd bought a box of cereal the night before, as well as two dozen eggs, a gallon of milk, a half-pound of butter, a loaf of bread, and stuff for lunch.

As they took the food out of the large communal refrigerator, Mallory saw they were not the only ones up early. A couple in their 20s quietly spoke German to one another as they worked at one of the stoves, and there was a small group of Japanese tourists sitting at a table in the adjoining dining room. Mallory found four mismatched bowls in one of the green cabinets and poured cereal for all of them at a table as close to the kitchen as possible, while Bob popped bread into a toaster and started scrambling up some eggs.

Mallory was surprised at how quickly Jupiter had transformed from the last one asleep to the one most fully awake. After cleaning up in the kitchen and putting everything back where it came from, the four of them went to their room, where Bob asked Jupiter what he wanted to find out.

He explained that he'd been wondering whether there had been any articles in the local newspapers about the Suleimans' intended gift to the Tri-Faith Center – and when both Bob and Mallory booted up their laptops, Mallory found something first.

A long and detailed article in the San Francisco *Chronicle* didn't tell them anything they didn't already know, but at the end of it there were readers' comments. As she read through them quickly, Mallory found nothing helpful until one comment almost blew the top of her head off.

"Good grief," she said aloud. "Listen to this. A woman named Sarah Willoughby wrote in. She claims she's a direct descendant of the English poet who translated the villanelles. She says she's hoping to visit the Center once it has the poems so that she can see the translations in her ancestor's own hand. I guess it's not *that* surprising. I mean, if the guy who translated the de Boissy poems lived hundreds and hundreds of years ago and had even two or three children, he'd have a lot of descendants by now. A *lot*. At least potentially."

"That's true," Pete said. "Remember me telling you up in Auburn about One Big Tree? That genealogy project where every human being on the planet would eventually be connected to every other one, through a sort of Human Family Tree?"

"You're both right," said Jupiter. "Still, it's great that at least one of Wilfred Willoughby's descendants lives in the Bay area somewhere and saw the article in the paper. Can you find an address for her? We should go visit her to see if she has any family stories. She might have heard something about the portfolio and could have a clue to what was in the secret pocket."

Mallory did a quick search and found

that Sarah Willoughby lived in Sausalito, in an area that seemed largely devoted to the docking of houseboats. In fact, the address Mallory found seemed to *be* the address of a houseboat. But since Sausalito and Alameda were in different directions from the hostel, and they were headed to Alameda with Father Samuel that afternoon, there was nothing much they could do right at the moment to get to know Sarah Willoughby better.

For that reason, when Bob asked what they should do until Father Samuel arrived, Pete said, "Why don't we check out that third labyrinth the woman in Grace Cathedral told me about? The one at Land's End. The only problem is how we'll get there."

"Maybe someone staying at the hostel is heading back into the city this morning and could give us a ride," Bob suggested. "We could ask at the reception desk."

"No," Jupiter said decisively. "We don't want to do that. We have to get back here in time for Father Samuel. If we go, we should hire a taxi or a car service so the driver will wait for us to be done and then bring us back here."

Mallory thought that was good thinking. When she looked up taxis and car services on her laptop, she found a car service with an office in Sausalito. When Bob called the number Mallory gave him, a woman picked up, very efficient and brisk, who told Bob that she'd have a car for them at the hostel in fifteen minutes. Would that be soon enough?

"Yes," Bob said, almost stammering. When he hung up the phone he was flustered.

"Yikes!" he said. "We better get going. The car will be here soon."

They gathered their belongings and went to wait in the parking lot. Not long after they got there, the car from Gillian's Transportation pulled up.

The driver was a woman who Mallory thought must be in her late twenties. She got out of the car and stood with her arms folded on her chest. Her face was sculpted, with high cheekbones and a square chin, and she was very handsome.

She wore a blue sleeveless shirt, revealing two well-toned arms with a tattoo of a hummingbird on the bicep of one of them. Her dark hair was short and spiky, as if she had jabbed at it with a scissors. She wore faded jeans and a pair of black boots that laced above the ankles. Mirrored sunglasses rested on the bridge of her nose, and light flashed at them as they approached.

She seemed a little tense as she took off her sunglasses and asked their names and what they did and where they were from and why they were in Sausalito, but by the time Jupiter had filled her in with the sketchiest of details, she had relaxed a bit.

"Investigators!" she said. "I've never driven a team of investigators around before. How long are you staying?"

"We don't really know," Mallory said. "Maybe two or three days."

"Well, if you need another ride after this one, be sure to ask for me by name. I'm Andie. Andrea McCorkindale."

McCorkindale! Mallory thought. An old Scottish name. Andrea of the Clan McCorkindale. Mallory had always liked women and girls like Andie, and when she said that they wanted to go to Land's End Park, Andie said she knew just how to get there − that she'd grown up in the city and knew it well, even though she now lived in Sausalito. They were quiet as they left the hostel, and within a few minutes they were back on the Golden Gate Bridge, headed into San Francisco.

Once they were in the city, Andie turned right onto California Street − the same street

Grace Cathedral was on but in the opposite direction. Not long afterwards, they arrived at the Land's End parking lot.

"You want me to wait?" Andie asked.

"That would be great," Jupiter said. "We won't be too long. We just want to see the labyrinth."

"The labyrinth?" Andie said. "Hold on. That's a pretty good hike, and hard to find. Do you want me to take you? Otherwise, I'm afraid you'll get lost."

"Would you?" Mallory asked.

Andie led the way through the park, which was sparsely populated with people Mallory supposed were tourists and with the street performers around whom small clusters had formed. It was good to have Andie with them as they passed a juggler wearing a fool's cap and tossing what looked like fireplace pokers into the air and a woman wearing a cape and top hat who was busy pulling multicolored scarves from her sleeves.

But soon they had left all that behind and were on a deserted trail heading west. The wind had picked up, and Mallory noticed how the coastal trees had been battered by salt and wind over years and years. They went down a flight of steps, turned to the right, walked along the sea cliff looking out over the Pacific, and finally reached an overlook from which they could gaze down on what they had come to see.

Fog still lingered out here at Land's End, and the sky was gray. The wind was constant and chilled her. After the beauty and tranquility of the labyrinth in the cathedral, Mallory found herself really disappointed. This one looked amateurish, crude, and irregular. Stones had been piled in lines to mark the path to the center.

Though the design did have eleven circles and thus resembled in its basic form the labyrinth at Grace, it was a poor facsimile. It looked like something a child might have made. Certainly nothing about it would cause you to contemplate the harmony of the universe.

No one gave any indication they wanted to go down to the labyrinth and walk it.

"Geez," Pete said. "This wasn't what I was expecting. At *all*. Sorry."

"Yeah," Andie said. "It's a little rugged and slapdash. But it's in a pretty terrific spot."

Mallory looked beyond the labyrinth to see the Pacific smashing against the rocks below before stretching to the horizon. And when she turned around she could see all the way up the Golden Gate Strait to the bridge they'd crossed. Andie was right. It *was* quite a spot.

The red spires of the bridge stood out sharply against the gray sky, and Mallory was once again astonished at what engineers like her father had managed to imagine and then build. Things far far better than this shoddy, semi-ridiculous so-called "labyrinth" made of rocks and pebbles. It was hard for Mallory to understand why anyone who had actually seen the one in Grace Cathedral would even try to *pretend* that this could be called by the same name.

As they all walked back toward Andie's car, Mallory found herself near Jupiter, and although the evening before had been very important to her, weirdly enough, she felt a little shy. In the normal run of a case, she almost never thought about the fact that she was a girl who had somehow been accepted into a boy's detective firm. But the talk last night with Jupiter, and the four of them all sleeping in the same room afterwards, had made her quite aware of it – and in a way that made her self-conscious. Why *couldn't* she have friendships with girls as well as boys? If nothing else, it would be nice to have another girl to talk to about Jupiter.

They made their way back along the path to the park, and though Mallory wasn't really much of a fan of street performers, she was cheered by the sight of other people enjoying them. When they ran across a mime entertaining a small crowd, she remembered Jupiter's comments about mimes quite clearly, but she thought that this one's routine was better than most.

Like most mimes, Mallory supposed, he was wearing white gloves, a black and white striped shirt, red suspenders, baggy black pants, and a beret. His face had been painted white, his lips red. Arched black eyebrows had been painted on his forehead. His eyes had been lined with kohl, and he had one black tear on each cheek.

He did a little jig, looked exaggeratedly sad, fell down, looked helpless, got up, tried to smile, and reached out imploringly. Andie – who had stopped and was standing next to Mallory – quietly said to her and the others, "This guy's actually a local celebrity. He was a down-on-his-luck actor who was caught running cons on tourists at some museum or other."

She snorted quietly.

"He calls himself Pierre Gaston, but his

real name is Joey Barton," she said. "He's actually quite famous around here as the ex-con mime."

Caught in the small crowd that had gathered, Mallory was distracted by a conversation between two people who obviously had seen Pierre Gaston before and who seemed to be fans, if such a thing could be possible.

Finally Jupiter groaned and asked if Pete and the others had seen enough.

"Sure," Pete said. "Let's go."

Mallory turned to follow them to Andie's car. She was just about to get in when she did a double take. Surely that Japanese girl on the edge of the crowd couldn't be Hiroka Ito, her only friend from the Scottish music and dance camp her mother had forced her to go to the summer before?

But the girl had Hiroka's hair and Hiroka's inimitably ironic expression. They'd written back and forth after they'd returned to their homes in Rocky Beach and San Francisco, but they lived so far apart that the correspondence had withered. Mallory had thought about writing to her before they came north, but she hadn't had time.

"Hiroka?" she said, tentatively.

"Mallory!" Hiroka said, turning and

rushing toward her. "What a surprise!"

It really *was* a surprise, Mallory thought. A very good one – and one that had arrived almost miraculously just when she was already wishing she had another girl to confide in!

7

Adam Suleiman

Bob had been thinking about how tedious, depressing, and annoying mimes were – how they abandoned the subtle possibilities of language for exaggerated expressions, larger-than-life gestures, and ridiculous literal-mindedness – when the Japanese girl suddenly appeared. He was surprised when Mallory called out to her, and even more surprised when the girl came over to greet her.

"I can't believe it's really you!" Mallory said as she and the girl embraced. The girl pointed to the mime and said something Bob couldn't catch, but which made Mallory dissolve into laughter.

"Guys," Mallory said, summoning Bob, Jupiter, and Pete. "This is the friend I've told you about from that Scottish music and dance camp last summer. Hiroka, these are The Three Investigators, Jupiter Jones, Pete Crenshaw, and Bob Andrews!"

So this was Hiroka Ito, Bob thought. He remembered Mallory telling him she lived in San Francisco, that her name meant "wise flower," and that she was always making Mallory laugh.

"I'm very glad to meet you," she said, shaking their hands. "Mallory told me so much about you in her letters."

"Do you live near here?" Bob asked.

"Actually," Hiroka said, "my family and I just moved to a houseboat in Sausalito. We're on the water!"

"Wow!" Pete exclaimed. "We were just reading about someone who lives on one of those houseboats. What's it like?"

"Pretty much like anywhere," Hiroka said, "but the floor tips. What are you guys doing here?"

"We're on a case," Jupiter said. "But we really can't talk about it much at the moment. If at all," he added.

"Maybe you can come visit me on the houseboat and tell me all about it," Hiroka said. "I'd like that."

She leaned in close to Mallory and whispered something that made her start to giggle. Bob was amazed. He'd never seen Mallory act remotely like this, though he had seen her laugh with Pete's girlfriend Califia.

"I wish we could talk with you now," Mallory said, "but we've got to get back to where we're staying. We have an appointment to see our new clients this afternoon. Let me get your information."

She pulled her cellphone out of her pocket and entered Hiroka's address and phone number in Sausalito.

"See you soon, wise flower," she said, slipping her cellphone back in her pocket. She seemed highly amused by her own joke.

Hiroka tilted her head, spread her fingers around her face like petals, and adopted an expression of serious ironic contemplation that made everyone laugh. It was a gesture such as a mime would make, but when Hiroka did it, it worked, Bob thought, because it made fun of mimes.

They were soon back at the hostel. "Thanks so much," Mallory said to Andie as they all piled out of her car. "We'll be sure to ask for you again if we need another ride."

"You do that," Andie said. "I enjoyed it. Maybe next time I drive you, I can run you by the Sausalito docks and show you the tall ships my girlfriend Phoebe helped to build. There's a ship called the *Matthew Turner* and one called the *Seaward*, and they're both really amazing."

"No!" said Pete in what seemed to Bob like total amazement. "I was just reading about those ships for a high school paper I'm writing. About Stephen Decatur, an early American hero who re-took the *Philadelphia* after it was captured by Barbary pirates!"

"I've heard of him! said Andie. "Well, gotta go!" she added, and they all waved as she zoomed off.

The morning expedition had taken longer than they'd planned for, so they quickly made lunch, then gathered their backpacks and important gear and went outside to await the arrival of Father Samuel. The sun was warm and they took shelter under a live oak. In no time at all, Father Samuel pulled up in the van and the four of them climbed in.

"Hello, hello," Father Samuel said. "I'm excited to have you meet the Suleimans."

"We are too," Bob said. And then they were off, back the way they had come the day before, through San Francisco and over the Bay Bridge, down through Oakland and over to Alameda. The ride took about forty-five minutes, though it was only about twenty-three miles.

As they drove through Alameda on their way to the Suleimans' house, Bob noticed that the neighborhood seemed calmer and quieter and a whole lot safer than most of the Bay

Area – more family-friendly. They passed numerous small parks and green spaces. The Suleimans lived on a tree-lined street.

The house itself was striking, with a red-tiled roof and arched doors and windows – clearly one of a kind, while a lot of houses they'd passed looked quite similar to one another.

"Here we are!" Father Samuel said, pulling into the driveway.

No sooner had they rung the doorbell than the door flew open. Bob knew immediately that the boy standing behind it was Adam Suleiman. He was very handsome, tall and slim, with coal-black hair cut short, almond skin, and flashing dark eyes. He gave off an aura of coiled intelligence and barely restrained excitement.

"The Three Investigators!" he said. "Welcome! Come in!" He backed away, bowing slightly, and the four of them trooped past him, followed by Father Samuel.

The interior of the house was decorated in warm colors and textures. The couches and chairs were upholstered in rich and subtle reds and oranges, and almost from the moment they entered, Mallory could not stop commenting on the rugs. They were clearly Middle

Eastern and might have been antiques, for all Bob knew, with symmetrical geometric designs that were bright, colorful, yet restful.

The rooms they walked through seemed both familiar and exotic to Bob – as though he had been here before, in another life. An intricately hammered copper tray, five feet wide, lay atop a delicate set of polished wooden legs. In fact, as Bob looked around, there were many copper pieces – in the dining room, a pierced copper and brass lantern hung over the table, and the buffet side piece held an arrangement of cooking pots. The rugs underfoot were so stunning that Bob wondered aloud whether they should really be walking on them.

"Of course!" said Adam. "That's what they're for!"

"Yes, yes," Father Samuel said, "a beautiful house, made with love. Adam, I presume you're taking us to meet your father."

"Yes," Adam said, "he's waiting for us outside."

In the center of the house was a tiled open-air courtyard with a low fountain that burbled happily in the afternoon sun and was surrounded by artfully arranged trees and shrubs in large earthenware pots.

Jacob Suleiman had been sitting in a

corner of the courtyard, but when he saw them, he came to join them. He had a book in one hand and he'd carefully placed his wire-rimmed glasses on his forehead. Bob would have known him anywhere as Adam's father. He had piercing brown eyes under gently curving brows, a thin mustache and goatee, and a sad, almost wistful expression.

Adam and his father seemed to Bob entirely American, though he knew that Mr. Suleiman had emigrated from Morocco, along with Adam's mother. Mr. Suleiman seemed more quiet and reserved than his son, but certainly friendly and welcoming.

"I've heard a lot about you," he said as he was introduced to the four of them. "Adam hasn't stopped singing your praises."

Adam beamed but also looked embarrassed. Bob could see that his enthusiasms were intense, and his focus ruthless.

"Mr. Suleiman," Mallory said, shaking his hand. "It's so great to meet a real architect. Your house is beautiful."

"Mallory's designing a new Headquarters for The Three Investigators," Pete said, "but she's keeping her plans a big secret."

Bob saw Mallory flash Pete a look that wasn't entirely friendly.

"Are you indeed?" Mr. Suleiman asked. "Do you plan to study architecture?"

"I'm not sure yet," Mallory said. Now she, too, was embarrassed, Bob saw. "I'm just starting out."

"I hope we have a chance to discuss your design," Mr. Suleiman said. "Adam, why don't you take your new friends to see your room before we talk about why they're here? When you're done, Father Samuel and I will meet you in the library."

"That's a good idea, Father," Adam said. Even from this brief interaction it was clear to Bob how close father and son were. Jacob's gaze was filled with benevolent pride.

Adam led the way back into the house and then down a hallway to a room that faced the courtyard and had double doors leading to it. Adam's bed was covered with a dark blue quilt. The rug on the floor was brown and rust, with medallions of blue and salmon. But what caught Bob's eye immediately was a drawing of the labyrinth at Chartres. It hung on the wall, beautifully framed in a dark highly varnished wood frame with hand-carved wooden rosettes at the four corners.

"Is that a drawing?" Bob asked.

"Yes," Adam said, nodding intently. "It

looks almost like a photograph, but it was done by hand by a French artist."

"It's gorgeous," Mallory said.

"Thank you," Adam said, "though I did nothing but hang it on the wall."

In the corner, Bob spied an interesting-looking three-legged Middle Eastern stool, with an embroidered fabric seat – perhaps part of an old rug – and an ingenious design that allowed the stool to fold up neatly for travel.

"Oh that!" Adam said, smiling. "Yes, my father brought that with him from Morocco. I take it with me when I go to Grace Cathedral in the city to study the labyrinth. I sit on it for hours, looking and thinking."

"How did your fascination with the labyrinth come about?" Jupiter asked.

"Because of the poems," Adam said. "I was always a great reader, and very interested in books. When I was about twelve I started looking through my father's library and I discovered the portfolio with the twelve villanelles. I was blown away by them. My father lost his religious beliefs not long after my mother died, but the poems really spoke to me.

"I started doing research on the labyrinth at Chartres, and when I found out that a replica was right here in the Bay Area, of course I had to go and see it. After that, I attended a service at the Cathedral, and then another. Soon I was going regularly. I loved the formal language − they were using the King James prayer book, which dates to 1611, not long after the villanelles themselves were written. And that's how I became a believer."

"Sort of like Saint Paul on the road to Damascus," Pete ventured.

Adam smiled. "Sort of. Though I can't say I felt I was struck by something like lightning. It happened gradually."

Bob was highly impressed with the clarity and logic of Adam's thought and language. He seemed a very mature fifteen-year-old − able to talk about his feelings and experiences without becoming emotional. Bob admired that. It was a skill he himself had not quite mastered.

Adam paused and looked a bit sheepish. "I have to tell you," he said, "what a huge fan of the four of you I am. Bob, your case reports are so vivid, and I love the way the four of you work together. Ever since I read about you using colored chalk to mark a route or leave a message, I've longed for the opportunity to do that myself. Not that anyone would know what it meant, of course. I've been telling my friends in school about you ever since I first found your website. I even told a few of them about having asked you to help out with this case!"

He laughed.

Bob was so pleased to hear Adam praise his reports that he didn't know what to say.

"Thank you very much for your faith in us," Jupiter said. "Perhaps you'd like one of our cards." He reached for his wallet.

"Yes!" Adam said, "I read about them in Bob's reports, but I've never seen one in person."

Jupiter handed a card to Adam who studied it. It read:

THE THREE INVESTIGATORS
"We Investigate Anything"
???
First Investigator – Jupiter Jones
Second Investigator – Pete Crenshaw
Records and Research – Bob Andrews

"Your names are printed in the colors of your chalk!" he said. "And I love the chimera logo – and the story of how you got it. But where's Mallory's name?"

Bob looked at Pete, who somehow managed to keep his face blank and not reveal what he and Bob and Jupiter all knew – that right at this moment, back at the hostel, there were cards with Mallory's name on them in the duffel bag which held their emergency equipment. Jupiter had brought the cards, the chalk, and the new helmet with him, in case they wanted to give them to her while they were up in San Francisco.

"I'm only a Special Consultant," Mallory said modestly.

"But we couldn't do without her," Jupiter said.

Adam carefully placed the card Jupiter had given him on a shelf, in front of a pile of books. "Now," he said, "it's time to show you the portfolio."

The library was a sanctuary at the far end of the house. Jacob Suleiman and the priest were sitting in comfortable chairs before an empty fireplace, but as Bob and the others entered, the men rose to their feet. The walls were lined with dark wooden shelves in which books, many of them very old, had been carefully arranged. Some had spines embossed with gold letters that shone in the dim room. A single enormous flat-weave rug with intricate designs in green and blue covered the floor.

The portfolio, stolen and now returned, was sitting on the tanned calfskin which had been inset over most of the surface of a large mahogany desk. The portfolio itself was closed, and next to it, in two piles, were the original villanelles in both the original French and the English translations.

"Please look at the portfolio carefully," Adam said, handing it to Jupiter.

Jupiter opened it and Bob saw immediately where the stitching had been snipped; as soon as Jupiter examined it Bob also saw the difference between the portfolio's front and back covers. The front was a thin leather-covered wooden board, but the back had two layers of leather, the secret pocket nestled between them.

"See how the stitching on the front and back is different," Adam said excitedly. "I can't believe I didn't notice it the very first time I looked at the portfolio. I even took pictures of it, and I feel very foolish that I didn't immediately see how it was constructed. The very feel of the thing suggests a secret hiding place."

"Yes," Jupiter said, thumbing the edge where the two sheets of leather were clearly visible. "I see what you mean."

"If we only knew what had been in the pocket – what has been removed," Adam said, "it would be so much easier to form a hypothesis about who had taken it. Perhaps it was a map of some sort, or some military information, or a secret message to the Pope."

Jupiter looked a bit surprised. "That's exactly what we thought," Jupiter said.

Bob was even more impressed when Adam went on to say it would be helpful to know if the poet's family had put some document there for the Pope's perusal, or whether it had been put there by someone else − perhaps the person who made the portfolio or someone who had access to it.

"This is quite amazing," Jupiter said, looking at Adam as though he'd just discovered a long-lost brother. "You've managed to reconstruct our thinking perfectly, but I'm sorry to say we've gotten no further than that."

"We do have one lead, though," Bob said. "We discovered that a direct descendent of the English poet who translated de Boissy's villanelles lives in Sausalito. Her name is Sarah Willoughby. Jupiter hopes she may know some family stories that would give us a clue as to what was in the secret pocket."

Jacob Suleiman looked startled. "My goodness," he said. "I know a woman named Sarah Willoughby just a little. She's a potter. I know her through Hakim Rahmani, my friend at the Tri-Faith Center, who hired her to throw several extremely large pots to plant trees in for the Center's courtyard. Like the ones in our courtyard."

"That's a remarkable coincidence," Jupiter said, pinching his bottom lip.

Or maybe not a coincidence, Bob thought. Maybe they were onto something with this Sarah Willoughby! On their last case, Pete had been quite eloquent about the fact that sometimes what looked like a coincidence was really evidence of the way in which all human beings were connected.

"I wonder if you could give us a little more background information," Jupiter went on. He turned to Mr. Suleiman. "For example, how exactly did you decide on the Tri-Faith Center as the place to which you wanted to donate the poems?"

"It was really my idea," Adam said. "When my father finally had the library inventoried and we discovered that we owned the only original handwritten copies of the poems in the world, I thought we ought to give them to an institution that had the resources to properly protect them and care for them – and where they could be studied as religious as well as historical documents.

"The Tri-Faith Center brings together Jews and Christians and Muslims," he continued. "Muslims – Barbary corsairs – originally stole the portfolio, but it ended up in the hands of Christians living in a Muslim country. So the Tri-Faith Center seemed an appropriate choice. Also, my father had designed the place, of course!"

"Here's another question," Jupiter said. "Did anything unusual happen between the time you announced the gift and the time the portfolio was stolen?"

"Well, yes, actually," Jacob said. "Not long after the gift was announced in the papers, I was contacted by an important French collector. He said I could basically name my price – he mentioned he'd be willing to pay enough to send Adam to four years of college and to establish a trust so that he could do anything he wanted with his life."

Wow! An honest-to-goodness suspect! Could the collector have been after the portfolio right from the start? Bob wondered.

"I've made a good deal of money as an architect," Jacob went on. "Still, I thought this was something I needed to consult Adam about. It was his life, after all, and the collector would obviously have taken good care of the poems. They'd already been available in printed form for three hundred and fifty years.

"But Adam wouldn't even consider it. He said no, right away. He wanted to give the poems to the world, not have them hidden away where only some rich man and his friends could look at them. He wanted other people to be able to see them and be as inspired as he was.

"I called my friend Hakim at the Center and explained what had happened. I told him I needed written reassurances about how the poems would be handled once the Center owned them. He was very understanding and had a set of binding promises drawn up. So I wrote to the collector and told him no."

"Could you repeat the name of your friend at the Center?" Bob said, taking out a notebook.

"Hakim Rahmani," Jacob said. "R-a-h-m-a-n-i."

"The Center has people from all over the world working there," Adam said. "Mr. Rahmani is Algerian, so he and my parents had a lot in common. Mr. Rahmani is a Muslim, like my mother was, before she converted.

"Now," Adam said, "let's look at the poems. I wish I could read them in the original French, like my father. The French occupied

Morocco for a long time and many Moroccans speak French. But Willoughby did an excellent job. He had to fit de Boissy's meaning into a very strict form."

"Why don't you read the first poem aloud, Bob?" said Father Samuel.

"Me?" Bob said, startled. "Aloud?"

"Of course," Father Samuel said. "Poetry is meant to be read aloud."

Bob picked up the top sheet of vellum, hundreds of years old, and stared at it. William Willoughby's handwriting was spidery but very readable. He saw that the poem was written in six three-line stanzas, except for the sixth stanza, which had four lines. The first and third lines of every stanza rhymed, throughout the poem, and all the second lines rhymed with one another. He cleared his throat and began.

A pilgrim cannot see what lies ahead;
The road ahead is anything but clear.
He lifts his feet and eats his daily bread.

A gorgeous flower at his heart is bled.
He walks within a highly ordered sphere;
A pilgrim cannot see what lies ahead.

"You see," Father Samuel said. "The

first and third lines alternate as the last lines of
the other stanzas all the way through."

Father Samuel nodded at Bob and he
began reading again.

His heart will fold to God like spooling thread;
He knows that one above him helps him steer.
He lifts his feet and eats his daily bread.

Each turning on the way may bring him dread.
His life is laid before him like a spear.
A pilgrim cannot see what lies ahead.

"You see?" asked Father Samuel again.
"The tension is between the pilgrim's fear and
God's certainty. As he walks, the pilgrim is
filled with dread, but God knows where he is
heading. Why don't you finish, Bob?"

Bob took a final breath. The experience
of reading a poem like this aloud was new to
him.

Still, over him the love of God is spread;
To him the path becomes a thicket dear.
He lifts his feet and eats his daily bread.

And at the end he sees the place he's tred.
The great cathedral calls to all who hear.

A pilgrim cannot see what lies ahead.
He lifts his feet and eats his daily bread.

Bob felt himself unexpectedly moved. His voice faltered as he tried to speak – but when Adam asked Bob whether he liked the poem, it was Jupiter who responded.

"Even scientists believe a kind of cosmic order ties the universe together," he said. "The kind of order that lets people create both villanelles and labyrinths."

"That's right," Adam said, looking at Jupiter keenly. "Bob wasn't exaggerating when he wrote about your intelligence."

Bob started to wince, afraid that Adam might use the dreaded word – what he and Pete referred to as "the g word" so that they never accidentally used the word "genius." But he needn't have worried. Adam was much too smart to do that. All he said was, "But for now, the big question is – what exactly was stolen from the portfolio's secret pocket? And how are we going to get it back?"

8

Kidnapped!

"Am I forgetting something?" Pete yelled. "What am I supposed to remember?" It was the next morning, and Pete and his friends were packing their backpacks for a day out.

"Just the regular stuff," Bob said.

"My bathing suit?" Pete asked. "After all, it's a houseboat."

"We won't be swimming," Jupiter said. "Not in Richardson Bay."

First they were going to visit Mallory's friend Hiroka − who Mallory had called the night before, after they'd gotten back from Alameda − and then they were going to drop in on Sarah Willoughby who they hadn't been able to contact. She wasn't answering her phone. They'd left a message on her answering machine, and they'd also sent her an e-mail, but she hadn't responded.

It turned out that she lived not all that far from Hiroka. In fact, Hiroka's family's houseboat and Sarah Willoughby's were moored at the same dock. Jupiter had asked Bob to write a brief letter to Willoughby intro-

143

ducing themselves. If she wasn't home when they went calling, they could leave the envelope with the letter in it for her to find later.

"Let's go!" Pete said. "I'm starving."

Since Hiroka had invited them for a late breakfast or an early lunch, so far today he hadn't eaten anything but a muffin and some bananas. He'd tried to sneak a bowl of cereal, but Bob had caught him and admonished him.

"You really shouldn't eat too much before going to someone's house for a meal," he'd said.

"I know," said Pete. "But I'd like to. Better safe than sorry."

When Bob called the taxi service and asked for Andie, the woman had said that she'd be there soon but that she wanted to warn them about something. Bob had his ear to his cellphone, and Pete couldn't hear what the dispatcher was saying, but when Bob said goodbye and clicked his cellphone shut, he reported back to the group.

"The dispatcher said it might take a little extra time for Andie to get from here to Hiroka's. We're only going about seven miles, but she said that some protest group or other has a lot of downtown Sausalito jammed up – including the area around the docks."

They went outside to wait, and it wasn't long before Andie pulled up in the same car she'd been driving yesterday.

"Hi guys," she said. "Ready for another adventure? Since we're paying a visit to some of Sausalito's famous houseboats, maybe on the way there I can drive you by the docks where the *Matthew Turner* and the *Seaward* are being moored. Even though Phoebe's the one who helped to build them, I'm as proud of them as it I'd built them myself!"

"But what about the protest group?" Bob asked.

"They're a pain in the ass and seem half-insane to me," Andie said. "But I should be able to get around them."

By this time, they'd left the headlands overlooking the Pacific and headed inland, toward Sausalito. The city was on Richardson Bay, an arm of San Francisco Bay. Pete had originally thought the houseboats were on the ocean side, but Bob had discovered that that was all protected federal land.

As for the tall ships, it seemed from what Andie was now saying that they were kept at some place called the Bay Model Visitor's Center Pier. Pete thought that was a strange name, but he was glad when Bob mentioned to

Andie that in two years Rocky Beach would be celebrating the 150th anniversary of its founding, and that his father had told Bob that he wanted to get a tall ship to Rocky Beach for the celebration.

"Why not one of Sausalito's?" Andie asked. "They go out and about all the time."

"I think my father is hoping for one of the ships at the San Diego Maritime Museum," Bob said. "Like the one Francis Drake sailed around the world in. The founder of Rocky Beach, Elijah Drake, believed that Francis Drake stopped there on his way up the coast of California."

"Whoa!" Andie said. "A real history buff! I love history myself. Maritime and military history especially. My grandfather worked at Sausalito Shipbuilding during World War II, building cargo ships for the U.S. Navy. And guess what? The place where the houseboats are now docked was where Sausalito Shipbuilding was located before it closed!"

Andie made good time until she got into Sausalito proper – where they came to a dead stop. There were barricades in the street beyond which was a mob of black-clad black-masked figures, their arms raised.

Andie looked back over her shoulder and

put the car in reverse. "I know how to get around this," she said. "If you can believe it, these freaks are trying to get a World War I memorial in the middle of Sausalito taken down by the city. Are they nuts? If you can't respect veterans who died in a war, you can't respect anything!"

Pete had to agree. Anyone who protested a World War I memorial would probably also protest Stephen Decatur taking the *Philadelphia* back from the Barbary pirates!

Now that they were moving away from the mob, Pete looked back over his shoulder at what seemed to be becoming a near-riot. The crowd had started throwing eggs and lighted firecrackers at cars driving by. It was impossible for Pete to understand why the people who took part in these so-called protest movements had to be so violent and angry and irrational. It wasn't as if this mob were protesting something reasonable – or something that was happening in the here and now.

The summer before, The Three Investigators had run into a similar group. They'd been visiting Pete's father on the set of *Bear Valley* – a movie he'd been working on about the soldier, explorer, senator, future presidential candidate, and world traveler John

Frémont. Pete mentioned this to Andie, at which she said, "I know about John Frémont! He named the entrance into San Francisco Bay the Golden Gate Strait because it reminded him of the Golden Horn of the Bosporus in Istanbul. That's why the bridge is called the Golden Gate Bridge."

"Why do protesters these days seem basically crazy?" Mallory said. "We saw some more of them last summer when we were at an art opening. A bunch of people protesting something or other decided to throw red and black paint on some artist's canvases. She was there, and she started crying."

"That seems a pretty tame response," said Andie.

Just then, Pete and the others saw some tall masts sticking up from what were clearly the two tall ships Andie's girlfriend Phoebe had helped to build. The sight was stirring, and even though The Three Investigators didn't really have time to get out of the car – especially after the delay with the protesters and their eggs and firecrackers! – Pete was still glad that Andie had driven them by here. They sat looking for about a minute, and then Andie drove them on to the Issaquah Dock area.

"Here we are," Andie said. "Sorry for

the delay with the protesters. Call me when you need me to come back – here's my private number." She handed Bob a card with her cell-phone on it. "I'll pick you up right away unless I'm on another job."

"See you soon," Pete said.

Issaquah Dock jutted into the bay, houseboats moored on either side of it. Apparently there were almost four hundred house-boats in Sausalito. As they searched for Hiroka's, they paused to look at the ones they passed. One had been painted a rich purple, with silver stars and moons around the door. A calico cat slept in the sun on the wood-shingled roof. Another was orange, with a wooden bar-rel in front, out of which spilled a tangle of red geraniums. Deep cobalt blues, trim painted fire-engine red, fuchsia and turquoise -- every-where there were fanciful colors.

But then Mallory saw Hiroka, down the dock, standing and waving.

"There she is," she said, and they hur-ried toward her.

"You made it!" Hiroka said. "I was wor-ried because of the demonstrations."

"The riots, you mean," said Pete. "As we were leaving, those people started throwing things. Luckily, the woman who was driving us knew a back way. This is so cool!"

"I'm glad you like it," Hiroka said. "Not everyone does." From her expression, Pete wasn't sure what side she herself was on.

She took them in to meet her mother and her sister Akemi – a child of about six.

"Her name means 'beautiful and bright,'" Hiroka confided. "She's pretty but I'm not sure about the bright part."

This made Mallory start laughing again. Pete was struck by how girlish Mallory seemed around Hiroka.

Mr. Ito was at work in the city, but Mrs. Ito hurried over to meet them. She was a bit taller than Hiroka, but still short, with a warm smile. Her long black hair was pulled back into a ponytail high on her scalp.

"I thought you might like a change," she said, "so I've made you a traditional Japanese breakfast."

Wow! Pete thought. That sounded exciting. He thought of some of the breakfasts his mother made, with chorizo and fiery chiles. He was sure this would be very different.

He was right. They all sat down together to what seemed to Pete like a very big meal – miso soup, steamed rice, grilled sea bass, and a type of pickled plum called umeboshi. There were other pickled vegetables, as well, and what he was told were fermented soybeans.

"This is like dinner!" Pete said.

"Yes," Mrs. Ito said, "but small portions. Better for you! No sugar!"

"Mom!" Hiroka said.

"Why did you move here to Sausalito, Mrs. Ito?" Jupiter asked after they'd started eating.

"Too expensive in San Francisco, and too crowded and dirty and dangerous," Mrs. Ito said. "This is much better."

It wasn't long before Mallory and Hiroka started talking about the Scottish music and dance camp they'd been to the previous summer. "Have you kept up with your Highland jig?" Hiroka asked, straight-faced.

"Na, me bonny lassie," Mallory said. "Ah haven't."

They both dissolved into laughter. Pete guessed you had to have been there. The boys were mostly quiet as the two girls talked about how silly the camp had seemed, and Hiroka remembered how good Mallory was at remembering things.

"There were these twelve huge flash cards, very confusing," Hiroka told the boys, "and Mallory remembered every one in the right order. And that's how we got our Nessies."

She left the table and returned with her model of the Loch Ness monster – identical to the one Pete had seen in Mallory's bedroom. But he'd never heard the story of how it had been won, and he was impressed all over again with Mallory's special talents.

Pete ate everything that had been put before him and loved it all – except for the umeboshi plum, which he thought was very salty and very sour, and the soybeans, which he'd decided to skip.

"So what is this case you're on?" Hiroka asked as they finished the meal and were sipping their cups of green tea.

"It involves some very old French poems," Mallory told her, "which were stolen and then returned."

"I see," Hiroka said. "It isn't a murder, then?"

Mallory laughed again. "No, but it's very interesting," she said. "In fact when we leave, we're going to go look for a woman named Sarah Willoughby who has a houseboat near here. She's descended from the English poet who first translated the French poems into English. You wouldn't know her, would you?"

Hiroka started to say something but stopped when her mother began talking.

"Sarah Willoughby?" Mrs. Ito said. "No. But we have certainly heard of her. The houseboat community is small, and everyone knows everyone else's business. We've heard she's a potter – quite good."

"Does she throw pots on her houseboat?" Mallory asked.

"No," Mrs. Ito said. "She has a studio with a kiln, somewhere in the outskirts of Sausalito, not too far away. From what I hear, she's there a lot, working, and then she's back on her houseboat for a while."

"But that's not all," Hiroka said. "You remember the mime at the park yesterday? Pierre Gaston? Or rather, Joey Barton? Well, I think he lives with Sarah Willoughby on her houseboat. At least I know she lives with a mime – I've seen one going in and out – and I'm pretty sure it's him."

That was weird, Pete thought. Why would anyone in their right mind want to live with a mime? But he guessed the guy had to live someplace. Still, it was also weird that a potter would live on a houseboat. Wasn't it?

Jupiter didn't look at all pleased with the idea that the woman they wanted to talk to might be living with a mime, and Pete wondered if he might even be having second thoughts.

No, that was ridiculous. Jupiter never had second thoughts – at least not about what to investigate during a case – and yet, when Mallory said, "I think we still need to talk to her," Jupiter looked unsure.

"There's no reason to think the guy lives in his mime makeup," Bob said. "Maybe he's a regular guy when he's not acting stupid. If we saw him without his makeup, we might not even recognize him."

"But you also might," said Hiroka. "If the guy who lives with Sarah Willoughby *is* Joey Barton, his picture has been in the paper. It seems that before he became a mime, he was an actor, and he was caught running cons on tourists."

"We already knew that, actually," Pete said. "Our taxi driver told us that yesterday!"

From there, the conversation turned to what Hiroka had been doing in the park where they'd met her the day before. As it turned out, she'd decided she wanted to be a journalist – "a skeptical journalist," as she put it – and this summer, she was interning for a small local paper.

"I pretended to be a journalist once," Mallory said to her. "At the end of last summer, when we were trying to get the goods on a dreadful German artist. But Bob's father *is* a journalist, and Bob sometimes thinks he might want to be one, too."

"Not really, any more," said Bob. "But what story were you working on in the park?"

"A story about street life in San Francisco," Hiroka said. "A lot of people are getting harassed and even hurt by the homeless population of the city, and I've been interviewing street performers to see how they're coping with the whole thing. I can't believe how scared they are to just say that they *are* scared. That a lot of the homeless people are mentally ill, and a lot of the others are drug addicts who'll do anything for a fix. A couple of street performers were beaten up and robbed in the park near Land's End last week."

"It's a bad situation," agreed Mrs. Ito. "But I wish Hiroka would stay out of San Francisco. She may want to become a skeptical journalist, but in the meantime, I'm a skeptical mother!"

Pete thought it was great that Hiroka was willing to tackle such a difficult subject, but at the moment he was more interested in Sarah

Willoughby and the mime she lived with. So when Hiroka volunteered to take them to Sarah Willoughby's houseboat after the meal was finished, he was psyched.

He and the others thanked Mrs. Ito, and she graciously invited them to come back whenever they wanted – though Pete knew that wouldn't happen any time soon. He liked the houseboat and the community it was in, but The Three Investigators and Mallory would be back in southern California as soon as the case was closed.

As Hiroka led the way to the houseboat where Sarah Willoughby lived, Pete was actually half-hoping the mime guy was there. He'd like to ask him a few questions. But when they got to where they were going, there was no one home. At least no one answered their repeated knocks.

Jupiter had thought ahead, as usual. Bob pulled out the envelope containing the letter he'd written and pinned it to the door.

"What does it say?" Pete asked.

"It's very general," Bob said. "I told her who we are and why we want to talk to her. I mentioned her comment in the paper and our meeting with the Suleimans. I gave her a bit more information than I left in the voice message or the e-mail. Also my phone number. And Mallory's."

"That's that, then," Hiroka said. "Can you come back to the boat for a while?"

"Gosh," Mallory said, "we'd really like to, but we'd better get going. We should call for our ride now and then walk you back."

Bob got Andie right away. "She's not busy," he reported. "She's on her way."

They were walking Hiroka back home, the five of them falling into an easy rhythm, joking around, when Bob's phone rang. He pulled it out of his pocket.

"It's probably Andie," he said, "saying she's having trouble getting to us because of those demonstrations."

But it wasn't Andie.

"Mr. Suleiman?" Bob said, surprised.

Pete could only hear what Bob was saying, but he could tell from Bob's face that whatever Mr. Suleiman had called him about must be very bad news.

"Oh no," Bob said. "When?" Bob's shoulders had gotten very tense, and he was frowning and shaking his head in dismay.

"What is it?" Pete said.

Bob glanced at him and shook his head and gestured with his hand not to talk.

"Tell us!" Pete said. He could feel his heart begin to beat more quickly.

"Don't worry," Bob said to Mr. Suleiman. "Or try not to worry. We'll be there as quick as we can. And so will the police, I'm sure.

Jupiter, Mallory, and Hiroka all looked horrified. Everyone wanted Bob to hang up so that he could tell them what was going on.

"O.K., Mr. Suleiman," Bob said. "We're on our way."

He hung up and looked at them with a grim expression.

"What?" Pete yelled.

"Adam Suleiman has been kidnapped," Bob said. "It seems that Jupiter was right to be worried about what San Francisco has become. Though nothing bad has happened to *us* here, something really bad has happened to Adam. He was walking down the block, away from his house, headed to downtown Alameda to run an errand, when a car pulled up and two guys dressed all in black and wearing black masks jumped out, shoved Adam into the car, and drove away," Bob said.

"Those protesters are kidnapping people now?" Pete exclaimed. "But why?" For the moment, the rest of them were speechless –

even Hiroka, who seemed almost as agitated as Pete was, and who was looking at the rest of them with alarm.

"Mr. Suleiman was looking out the window watching Adam when it happened and he managed to whip out his cellphone and take a picture of the car. That's one good thing," Bob said. "The only one I can think of. And Alameda itself actually seemed pretty safe."

"Did Mr. Suleiman get the license plate number?" Jupiter asked.

"No," Bob said. "And he didn't get the men either. Just the car. It happened about twenty minutes ago! He's called the cops, and they're on their way, but Mr. Suleiman said he knows that Adam would have more faith in us than in the police, and he wants us on the case as soon as possible."

"I do, too," Jupiter said. "We'll have Andie drive us right over to Alameda. Did Mr. Suleiman have any other thoughts?"

"Yes," Bob said. "He doesn't know whether the kidnapping has anything to do with the theft and return of the portfolio, but it seems a bit of a coincidence if it doesn't. Frankly, I don't think it *was* the protesters — even if they were dressed the same."

"I agree," Jupiter said. "Call Andie

again and see if you can do anything to speed her up. Tell her there's been a kidnapping."

Bob got Andie who said again that she was on her way but that the protest seemed to have spread and that she thought it might be even harder to get through town quickly. Luckily they were on the north end of Sausalito, and she thought she'd take them north to San Rafael and then over the Richmond-San Rafael Bridge and down the east side of the bay. It would be quicker.

"We better get down to where Andie dropped us off," Pete said.

As they hurried back there, Mallory said to Hiroka, "I hope I see you again, sooner this time. Maybe you can come down to Rocky Beach and visit us."

"I'd really like that," Hiroka said. "One of these summers I'm actually hoping to get an internship with Dissident News. They have a program outside Los Angeles which lets high school seniors, or recent high school graduates, do video reports on YouTube. Good luck with your case. Call me if I can help you out. I'm really shocked. I can't believe how bad things are getting these days."

"I can't, either," said Mallory. She hugged Hiroka, hard.

Andie arrived not long after, and they said goodbye to Hiroka and climbed into Andie's car.

"A kidnapping?" she said. "That sounds really serious."

She took a left down a side street. "Uh-oh," she said. Ahead of her was a black-clad mob coming toward them. She threw the car in reverse and tried to turn around, but the mob was too fast.

Pete watched as the members of the mob surrounded the car. Before they got there, he and the others managed to lock the doors and roll all the windows up. Though he didn't normally feel claustrophobic, Pete felt totally penned in by this crowd. Andie tried to move the car forward, inch by inch and was making some progress when a bunch of apparent lunatics threw themselves onto the car. One seemed to be swimming across the hood, toward the windshield, his fiendish eyes the only thing visible through his black mask.

"Get off!" Pete yelled. "We're in a hurry. Someone's in trouble!"

He pounded with his fist on the interior of the windshield, and the guy on the hood pounded back. It looked to Pete as though he was trying to break his way into the car. He was joined by other rioters – this was definitely a riot now – on either side of the car. They began pummeling the windows with their fists.

What if someone had had a heart attack or was having a baby? Pete wondered. People shouldn't be allowed to block public roads and stop cars like this. It was dangerous! And Adam Suleiman had been kidnapped. A great guy was in trouble, and they were trying to help, and these goons were keeping them from it. Where were the Sausalito police? This would never have happened in Rocky Beach, Pete thought. And it shouldn't happen anywhere in America!

Andie leaned on the horn, long and loud, and the crowd outside raised their voices even higher.

Geez! Pete thought. What were they going to do?

9

Ghost-to-Ghost Hookup 2.0

As Jupiter thought about it afterwards, the whole scene was a blur of black masks and screaming and Pete yelling and Andie stepping on the gas in fits and starts and finally the crowd opening up and Andie gunning it, and before too long they were headed north on 101, and then east on the five-and-a-half mile Richmond-San Raphael Bridge. But while it was going on, it was as if time had stopped, and there was a moment when Jupiter thought it actually had.

He found the screaming and the pounding both so pointless and so disorienting that, although he was trying hard to think like a rational human being, at the time all this was happening he found his mind a blur – simultaneously angry and frightened at the actions of the black-clad figures around the car.

Angry because they wanted to interfere with his freedom and frightened because he was afraid that they might succeed. Their actions seemed aimed not at protest but at destruction. This was terrible, pointless violence,

163

and as the very long moment he was in seemed to stretch to forever, Jupiter thought about what Andie had told them about the World War I Memorial in downtown Sausalito. To Jupiter, the protesters' actions were incomprehensible. Although no one wanted wars, they were a part of human history, and remembering the people who had died in them was a human obligation.

The truth was, more and more people these days simply seemed to want to erase the past — or at least human beings' knowledge of it — and yet, as Thomas Aquinas had said, in a different way, there was no way to plan a productive future without remembering what had happened in the past. Jupiter had never been easily intimidated, but a mob like this one would intimidate anyone. Mobs and the kinds of accomplishments reported in *Human Achievement Through The Ages* were on opposite ends of the spectrum, he thought.

At last Andie arrived at the Suleimans. Two police cruisers had pulled up to the curb, their lights flashing. Jupiter, tense but alert, could see that the four officers were just now leaving the house as he and the others thanked Andie and told her they'd call for her later.

"Thank goodness you're here," Jacob

Suleiman said as he welcomed them into the house. His face was pale, and he rubbed his hands together as if they were cold. "There's news. After I contacted Bob but before the police arrived, one of the kidnappers called. He told me that Adam's safe."

"Did you recognize the voice?" Jupiter asked. "I've read that most kidnappers are people known to the family."

"No," Mr. Suleiman said. "He muffled it. Probably just a piece of cloth over the receiver, no distorter or synthesizer. But he had a strange French accent, and he said he'd bring Adam back safely in exchange for the portfolio of poems."

"Maybe it's the collector you said no to!" Bob said. "Or someone he hired."

"It sure doesn't sound like the protesters," Pete said.

"It's too early to speculate," Jupiter said. "Anything else?"

"He said he'd be in touch with a plan for how he'd get the ransom," Mr. Suleiman said. "He specifically mentioned that we wouldn't be meeting on a deserted road, or anything like that. After he got the poems, he'd release Adam."

He paused and looked stricken. "He said

Adam would be quite safe for a day or two, but that if they didn't get the portfolio in exactly the manner they prescribed, he might not be so safe any more."

"There's no need to worry," Jupiter said, trying to be consoling though he found the details alarming. "That's the threat all kidnappers make."

"Of course," Mr. Suleiman said, "my first impulse was just to give them the poems immediately, but the police advised me that might not be wise. The sergeant said they'd be back with equipment to monitor and trace any calls that come in."

Jupiter was impressed with how calm Mr. Suleiman seemed – how he was capable of telling them what had happened in a logical fashion in spite of his quite visible distress.

"Come with me," he said, beckoning to them as he walked away. "I want to show you the picture I took of the car."

Jupiter and the others followed Mr. Suleiman to his study, which they hadn't seen before. It was smaller than many of the other rooms, or seemed so. There was a worktable with furled blueprints on it, and in the corner an industrial-sized copy machine. They all crowded behind his desk on which a computer and large display were arranged. He'd already downloaded the photo from his phone to the computer.

"I gave the photo to the police, of course," Mr. Suleiman said. "They're going to post it on their website and X feed and give it to the local television stations."

Jupiter knew that X was a popular social media site which had once been called Twitter but he knew next to nothing about how it worked. As he looked at the picture of the kidnapper's car, his first reaction was disbelief. It was an old mostly-yellow sedan, battered and rusty, with a broken taillight – a junker of a kind rarely still on the road.

Jupiter wondered how it could possibly have passed inspection in the state. Its muffler was about to fall off. The rear passenger side door had been painted a rusted orange, as if primer had been applied and the job never finished. In fact, the car looked like it had had several bad paint jobs, and on the trunk someone had hand-painted a smiley face with a thick red tongue hanging out. There wasn't another car like it in the entire country, Jupiter thought.

"Holy moly!" Pete said.

"That should be pretty easy to locate," Mallory said. "It's more distinctive than Rafael

Solares's pick-up – or even Connor's junker!"

"That's true," Bob said. "It's probably the most recognizable car in northern California. Why would anyone use a car like that instead of one that looked like every other car on the road?"

As Jupiter stared at the photograph, he was afraid there was only one reasonable answer.

"My guess is that the kidnappers are using it as a decoy," Jupiter said. "They've probably already ditched it for something a good deal more invisible. The police will be off on a merry chase for something that will have nothing to do with Adam. The car is so old and cheap the kidnappers don't care if they never see it again. In the meanwhile it'll buy them some time while the authorities look for it. Nevertheless, if we can locate it, we'd have a concrete place to start."

"I see why Adam was so impressed with The Three Investigators," Mr. Suleiman said.

"Maybe there'll be fingerprints when they find it," Pete said hopefully.

"I doubt it," Jupiter said. "Adam's fingerprints, maybe, but I'd bet the kidnappers wore gloves as well as masks."

Mr. Suleiman sat down heavily in his

desk chair. It seemed that everything that had happened had finally caught up with him. He looked distraught, and he covered his mouth with the palm of his right hand, as if trying to keep his feelings from escaping. He shook his head wearily.

"I wish now Adam had never had the idea of giving the poems to the Center," he said. "No one even knew we had them. And if it hadn't been for the fact that the Center wanted to announce the gift in the papers, none of this would have happened, either. At least we could have kept it a secret until after the poems were delivered."

"It does no good to second-guess yourself," Jupiter said. "You'll just get more upset with all the what-ifs. Even if the Center hadn't wished to announce the gift, surely people who worked there knew about it, and there's no way of knowing whether everything that's happened wouldn't have happened anyway as a result of word of mouth."

Jupiter was happy to see that this calmed Mr. Suleiman down and seemed to relieve his mind.

"You said that the police were going to post your photograph on their X feed," he added. "How many people would that normally reach? Do you know, Bob?"

Bob took a seat, pulled out his laptop, and checked. "There's no way to figure out their Internet traffic," he said, "but they have about 4500 people following their X account."

"I wish I better understood how this X thing works," Jupiter said. "Although 4500 sounds like a lot of people, I wonder if it's enough to generate a specific result – in this case the identification of the car."

"You're right," Bob said. "Forty-five hundred followers isn't a lot – not considering how X works. People following the Alameda police would only see the post with the photo if they were looking at their own account when the picture was actually posted, or shortly thereafter. Otherwise it would get buried by other stuff streaming in, and they'd probably never see it at all. Besides, the police have a lot to do and I doubt this is going to lead to anything."

This was what Jupiter had feared, and he was about to go on to something else when Bob said, "But there *is* a way we might be able to get the photo to a lot more people."

"What is it?" Jupiter said.

"The other day I was wondering if any of the people we've gotten to know through our cases had X accounts," Bob said, "and if so, how many followers they had. So I looked them up. You may not believe this, but well over a million people follow both Daman Dawalia and Odetta Dharmapuki. Maybe they'd help us by posting the picture of the junker car. With several million people, I think there'd be a better chance that someone had seen it."

"That's an *excellent* idea," Jupiter said. "Good thinking, Records! I'm sure both Daman and Odetta would be willing to help us out, especially in such a good cause."

"In a way, it's just a newer version of the Ghost-to-Ghost hookup," Bob said. "More technologically advanced and a lot faster than phone calls or e-mail. And this case is actually very much like the first time we ever used the hookup – when we were looking for a car in the mystery involving the stuttering parrot."

"A *lot* faster," Pete said. "Back then we had to call people and ask them to each call five more people, and so on. And *that* worked. So this will work even *better*, even if lots of people drop the ball!"

"That's right," Bob said. "If we had a potential pool of, say, three million people looking within the next two hours, I bet we'd get results."

"Let's get to work," Mallory said.

"And we can add in everyone we know," Bob said. "We can ask Connor O'Malley and Cornelius Patterson and Ivan and Cassandra Fedorov, and anyone else I'm forgetting at the moment."

"Why don't the four of you get to work out in the shady part of the courtyard?" Mr. Suleiman said. "I'll stay in here waiting for any further calls or contacts."

"Don't forget to send us an e-mail with the photo you took of the car," Bob said.

"Of course," Mr. Suleiman said. "Right away." He took them from his study to a set of doors leading to the courtyard and showed them a table and a set of chairs where they could comfortably work.

Jupiter soon got an education in X from Bob, who suggested that the very first thing they should do was set up their own account – a Three Investigators X account – so that they could follow the people whose help they'd be asking.

"How do you do that?" Jupiter asked.

"Like this," Bob said. With a few key-strokes he had established an account. "Now we need a description of ourselves for the profile."

"Profile?" Jupiter asked.

"Just a short statement at the top that lets people know who we are. How about 'We're Jupiter Jones, Pete Crenshaw, Bob Andrews, and Mallory MacLeod, and We Investigate Anything'?"

Pete took a look. "Add three question marks," he said decisively.

"Done," Bob said. "Now, all we need to do is to write a pithy post or two, then send an e-mail to the people we're following asking them to follow *us* — and then resend our posts."

Under other circumstances, Jupiter would have been amused to find himself dealing with something that had once been called Twitter, but was now called X, but as it was, he wasn't, and as Bob began compiling a list of all the people they knew with X accounts, he had to admit that Bob had been right — it was the good old Ghost-to-Ghost hookup in a brand-new form.

As Bob got to work, Jupiter saw that, although they would only be following about ten people, and as of yet had no followers themselves, the people they were following had lots of followers. Cassandra Fedorov had 200, her husband Ivan had 3000, Cornelius Patterson,

Lyle Smith's partner, had 300, Connor O'Malley had 800, Daman Duwalia had a million and a half, and Odetta Dharmapuki had over two million.

"O.K.," Bob said. "We're all set. Now we need to write an urgent message to the people we want help from. The only trick is that it has to have fewer than 280 characters."

"What?" Jupiter said. "Why?"

"To keep people from going on too long, I guess," Bob said, "and I think because originally there was some technical limitation."

Mallory had already starting working on her computer. After a minute or two she said, "How about this?"

"What have you got?" Jupiter asked.

"Please help us rescue 15-year-old Adam Suleiman," Mallory read, "who was walking away from his house in Alameda this morning when two masked black-clad thugs forced him into this car. His father managed to photograph it through his kitchen window."

"What does that add up to?" Pete asked.

"Two hundred forty-seven characters, with spaces," Mallory said.

"That's great!" Pete said. "That sure got *my* attention."

"Bob can attach the photograph to that

one, which focuses attention on the car," Mallory said, "and then maybe we can follow it up with a second one that reads, 'The kidnappers demand ransom, which Adam's father is more than willing to pay, but the police have warned that Adam may be injured, so if you have seen this car ANYWHERE, please let us know where and when at once!'"

"That should work," Bob said approvingly.

Jupiter was impressed with how simple and clear the messages were, and once she had rigorously checked them for typos, Mallory sent them to Bob, who put them together with the photograph he'd gotten from Mr. Suleiman and then uploaded it to the brand-new Three Investigators X account.

Bob explained that, since they had no followers yet, no one but they themselves would actually see the post – but if Daman Dawalia and Odetta Dharmapuki re-posted the messages, they'd reach almost four million potential sets of eyes.

"So how do we get the people we're following to send our message out again?" Pete asked.

"We need to send an e-mail to Daman and Odetta and the others," Bob said. "In the e-mail we'll ask them to follow us and to help us with our case by re-sending the posts that Mallory wrote. We'll include a direct link to our messages to make it easy for them.

"All they have to do is click on the link, and when our message opens, to send it out again – hopefully asking the people who are following them to do the same thing. We could get ten million people involved in no time. Daman's and Odetta's fans would probably love to do something they asked them to do."

Although Jupiter had never before considered using social media, he found himself oddly excited by the idea that The Three Investigators could enlist ten million people to help them with the click of a mouse. He watched as Bob and Mallory collaborated on an e-mail they could send to everyone they were following and then as Bob sent the e-mail out with the links to their messages. Everyone applauded when it was done, and Pete went around high-fiving everyone. Then they settled down to wait.

Jupiter had no idea how long it would take for something to happen, and his natural skepticism kicked in, but as the four of them stared at the open screen of Bob's laptop, little dings started sounding.

"What's that?" he asked.

"We're getting responses," Bob said. "Look!"

Less than ten minutes had passed since Bob had pressed SEND on the e-mails, and Jupiter watched in excited amazement as – BAM BAM BAM BAM BAM – he saw that five of the people they'd written to had re-sent their messages. The re-sends were coming into The Three Investigators account because they'd been the original senders. And happily Daman, with his one and a half million followers, was one of the people who'd responded at once!

Jupiter was filled with a rush of triumph. This might really get results! he thought. The four of them had worked together, and, less than a half hour after they'd gotten to the Suleimans, real progress was being made.

It took some time for Odetta to get her e-mail and to respond, but Jupiter was just as thrilled to see that she'd re-sent their message as he'd been to see Daman do it, and to his great excitement and that of his friends, replies started flooding in.

"Yes!" Pete yelled, thrusting his fist into the air. "We've got this!"

They broke into two teams, Bob and Jupiter on one with Bob's laptop and Pete and Mallory on the other with hers, and they began to read through everything that was flooding in, looking for people who had information they could use.

Almost at once Jupiter saw the downside of X. Most of the messages they got had nothing to contribute at all, just a lot of good wishes and tiny pictures smaller than a pea that Bob said were called emoticons.

"Emoticons?" Jupiter said.

"For people who don't trust their ability to convey emotions with language," Mallory said. "Don't you hate them?"

It was depressing how many messages were a waste of time – "Good luck!" and "I hope you find him soon!!" and "Haven't seen the car but our prayers are with you!!!" and "Ugh! Masked black-clad thugs!!!!"

Far worse were the ugly nasty ones, and Jupiter quickly saw that there were lots of people in the world who wished nothing but harm on their fellows.

"Bet it served him right!" someone wrote. "I have a list of people I'd like to see kidnapped." And "If his father can afford the ransom, then he has too much money!"

More than depressing, these messages were disgusting and, Jupiter thought, almost a reason to never visit X again. He wondered what had gone wrong in American society that was making it so easy for this kind of nastiness to flourish.

Of course – looked at in a certain way, at least – the people on X were just exercising their right to speak freely – a right enshrined in the First Amendment to the American Constitution. But although most human beings were a mix of kind and selfish impulses, there seemed to be something about the current moment in human history which was encouraging the selfish impulses and discouraging the kind ones.

Still, the thing that really bothered him as he read the posts flooding into their brand-new X feed was that so few of the people who were writing them seemed to have been educated as to the truly amazing things you could do with language – or even what language was really for. While Jupiter wasn't interested in writing the same way Bob was, he'd always been careful to be as precise as possible – something the people that were writing now definitely weren't being.

Still, hidden among all the badly written or stupid or pointless messages was some actual information.

"Saw that car yesterday at the Safeway

in the Mission," someone wrote. Another wrote, "Saw it this morning on the 580."

Maybe this will work after all, Jupiter thought. He mentally crossed his fingers and kept on reading.

10

A Plan Takes Shape

Four hours later, Bob and the others were totally exhausted and ready to return to the hostel for the night. Bob had called Andie, but she was back in Sausalito when he reached her and said it would take at least half an hour and probably more to pick them up.

It had been an eventful time. The police had arrived a few hours earlier to install their surveillance equipment on Mr. Suleiman's phone. They'd given him lots of instructions and told him they'd leave a cruiser with two uniforms outside on the street.

They seemed quite annoyed to have The Three Investigators around, asking questions, but when Mr. Suleiman said they were friends of the family, there was nothing the police could do or say. They'd been gone now for about an hour – all except for the cruiser lurking on the curb.

When the police had first arrived, Bob and the others had abandoned their table in the courtyard and joined Mr. Suleiman in the house. He dealt with the issue of surveillance on his phone in an amazingly calm manner, but when the police asked for additional photographs of Adam, his calm had started to crumble. To Bob's surprise, when the police were finally gone, Mallory asked Mr. Suleiman if he could show her any pictures he had of Adam as a child.

Although Pete was normally the one who was most sensitive to people's emotional needs, this time, it seemed that Mallory was stepping up to the plate.

While Pete and Bob and Jupiter went back to work at the table in the courtyard, Mallory closed her computer and went to sit with Jacob Suleiman in a couple of nearby chairs while he showed her pictures of Adam as a baby, a toddler, and a little boy.

Although Bob was close enough to hear the conversation, he was also reading X posts and trying to graph possible sightings of the kidnapper's car on an online map, so he wasn't certain how Mallory and Mr. Suleiman had gotten onto the topic of architecture, but he could tell from the tone of Mr. Suleiman's voice that it was taking his mind off Adam's kidnapping.

Mallory kept asking him questions about when he had first decided he wanted to be an architect, what kinds of things he had studied in school, and so on, and the more he talked, the more relaxed and focused he sounded.

At some point, as Bob listened with half an ear, he heard Mr. Suleiman ask Mallory about Pete's comment of the day before – that Mallory was designing a new Headquarters for The Three Investigators – and soon they were talking about hip roofs, and cupolas, and dormers, and a lot of other stuff that seemed very technical to Bob, but that both Mallory and Jacob Suleiman seemed to find fascinating.

As the information Bob and his friends were analyzing began to pile up, and the online map didn't seem adequate to the task of keeping it organized, Bob had had the idea to ask Mr. Suleiman if he could give them an actual map of Alameda and the surrounding area, and Mr. Suleiman had gotten to his feet and led the way first to the library and then to his study.

In the library, he'd pulled out several large volumes, and when he'd found a detailed map of the area they were interested in, he'd taken it to his study and made a significantly enlarged copy on his architectural copy machine. They'd brought these copies back to the dining room, where Bob and Mallory had also brought their computers.

As the five of them sat around the dining room table before an enormous blowup of the part of California they were trying to map – an area within a four-hour drive of Mr. Suleiman's house – Jacob Suleiman himself marked down the places where people had seen the car with a small red dot.

The best information The Three Investigators had gotten came in the form of GPS locations. There had been clusters of sightings on Webster Street in Alameda, in Oakland on the Interstate, and then on California State Highway 24 in Temescal and Upper Rockridge and on up to Orinda.

As Mr. Suleiman mapped the sightings, the route the car had taken became clear. A river of red dots streamed from Alameda to Danville – but just as they were about to discuss this route in detail, the doorbell rang.

Looking out the window, Mr. Suleiman said, "It's Father Samuel. I called him after the police left to tell him what had happened. I asked if he'd be willing to stay with me tonight."

He got to his feet and went to the door.

"Jacob," the priest said falteringly after embracing his friend. "Have no fear. God is with you, and with Adam."

But as Mr. Suleiman led the priest into the dining room, Bob could see that Father Samuel looked profoundly shaken. His white hair was disheveled, and he kept fingering a rosary, dropping it, and then picking it up again.

Although Jacob Suleiman had been both calm and focused during the process of mapping the kidnapper's car, all of a sudden, with the arrival of Father Samuel, he was anything but calm.

"I wish I believed that," Mr. Suleiman said to him. "To tell you the truth, this is the first time I've felt like praying since Zahra died."

This almost undid the priest. He put his hand on Jacob Suleiman's shoulder. "God is always there and listening, my son, whether you believe in Him or not," he said. "You shouldn't hesitate to pour out your heart to Him. It will do you good."

"No, it won't," said Mr. Suleiman. "What's been doing me good has been talking to these young people, and having them help me. Look at this map, Samuel. Those red dots all mark places where the car Adam was taken away in have been sighted in the last few hours. The Three Investigators have set up a social media account and sent out a picture of the car."

"This is a miracle," Father Samuel said, looking at the map.

"In a way," Mr. Suleiman said. "Mostly it's a testament to our young friends' ingenuity and hard work."

Making a visible effort to shake off the gloom the old priest had brought into the house, Mr. Suleiman said to Jupiter, "So you think Adam's in Danville?"

"It's hard to know," Jupiter replied. "As you can see, the sightings simply stop right outside of the town."

"It's weird," Pete said. "It's almost like the car just *disappeared*. Like aliens just sucked it right into their spacecraft."

Mr. Suleiman looked grim. "I don't think Adam's in outer space. But it *is* rather strange that the trail runs cold in Danville."

"I wonder if they could have turned off and headed up toward Mount Diablo?" Bob said, looking at the area to the east of the place the red dots came to an end.

"The Devil's Mountain," Father Samuel said, shaking his head almost fearfully. "I feel as if this is my fault. All of it. If I hadn't —"

Bob thought the priest wasn't really helping. "What I mean," he said to Mr. Suleiman, "is that the area around there is all state or federal land, without any real population. Look at all those switchbacks." He pointed to the convoluted twisty turns of the route to Mount Diablo State Park.

"Nothing but campsites and hiking trails," he added. "I doubt there's even any Internet access, so anyone who might have seen the car probably didn't even get any of the X messages."

"That could explain it," Jupiter said. "And if so, perhaps they'll be posting something later on."

"Maybe," said Bob. "But I get the impression that in a case like this whatever is going to happen with X either happens immediately or doesn't happen at all. In that way, it's a little bit different from our original Ghost-to-Ghost hook-up. Still, I'm amazed at how well it's worked so far. I'm also surprised. I thought it would be numbers that would help us −− the millions of followers of Daman Duwalia and Odetta Dharmapuki − when it was actually geography."

"What do you mean?" asked Jacob Suleiman with interest.

"Well, unless I'm wrong," Bob said, "it

was the local people – our friend Connor O'Malley especially – whose followers came through for us. Connor is an artist who lives in Auburn, and as it turns out, he has contacts in the whole area between Auburn and San Francisco."

"That's fascinating," said Mr. Suleiman. "You already seem to understand this platform pretty well."

"Actually, I've been thinking about it for a while now," Bob explained. "In fact, before Father Samuel even contacted us about the secret compartment in the portfolio, I was saying to my father that I thought that maybe The Three Investigators should find a way to use social media. He wasn't so sure."

He paused. "Mr. Suleiman, when we leave, we're going to want to take this map with us," he said. "Maybe you should make a couple of copies of it first – one to keep for yourself, and one to give to the police."

"That's an excellent idea," Mr. Suleiman said. "I'll be back in a minute." He carefully rolled up the map.

Once he was safely out of the room, Jupiter turned to Bob.

"Social media mobs *are* a menace," he said seriously. "But before today, I never imagined that anyone would write an approving comment about a violent abduction. Something has really gone wrong with a society in which that sort of thing can happen without public condemnation."

"Someone wrote that they approved of Adam's kidnapping?" asked Father Samuel, sounding stricken.

"Not exactly," Jupiter responded. "But someone did write that if his father could afford the ransom, he had too much money."

"Oh, dear," said Father Samuel. "I really *can't* help feeling it's all my fault." He wrung his hands together, then thrust them into pockets in his cassock.

That was the second time Father Samuel had said this.

"Why are you saying that, Father? *You* didn't kidnap Adam!" Pete said.

"No," the priest admitted. "But I *did* – well – encourage Jacob and Adam to give the poems to the Tri-Faith Center, and I also – "

Just then, Jacob Suleiman came back into the dining room with the original marked map. Overhearing the priest's final comment, he said, "Adam didn't require any encouragement, Samuel, as you well remember."

"Maybe not," Father Samuel said. He

paused, twisting his hands again. "Why don't I make you some supper? You must keep up your strength."

"That's good of you, Samuel," Mr. Suleiman said, "but I couldn't eat a thing. Perhaps our friends – ?" He turned to Bob and the others.

"We're not hungry either," Pete said immediately. "But thank you. We need to get back to our hostel."

Bob smiled. He knew Pete was probably starving, but his kindness and good sense came first – and in a little while, the doorbell rang again. This time, it was Andie.

Bob and the others said good night to Mr. Suleiman and Father Samuel. "Now call me any time, day or night," Mr. Suleiman told them. "Don't worry about waking me. I want to know whatever you find out, at once."

"We will," Bob assured him.

Back in the car, Bob and the others told Andie everything they knew so far. "The car just disappeared?" she said.

"Well," Pete said. "You know. We're sure it didn't really disappear. It's just that after a certain point, no one saw it again. No one."

"That's pretty odd," Andie said. "But maybe they just got to where they were going."

"But it's just a spot on the highway," Mallory said.

"I see what you mean," Andie said.

Bob was so tired that he nodded off on the way back to Sausalito. Mallory had asked Andie to stop at Seong's Market again. They needed to make dinner, and since Bob was a little rested after his nap, he was deputized to come up with something reasonable and simple. Once again, the subject of the trucking company California Bounty came up in the conversation with Mrs. Seong.

Back at the hostel, they all gathered in the kitchen. While Mallory and Jupiter cut up peaches, plums, and bananas for a fruit salad, Pete sliced tomatoes and avocados and arranged them on a plate.

Bob had learned to cook from his mother, so he cooked some zucchini, then plopped some chicken cutlets into flour and quickly fried them, and soon they were sitting together at a table in the dining room and eating ravenously.

All of them but Jupiter – who said that, before too much more time passed, he wanted to make a few obvious points.

"First," he said, "it's safe to conclude that whoever stole the portfolio and then left it in Grace Cathedral is not one of the men who kidnapped Adam. Since what they want is the portfolio, they'd never have returned it if they'd been the ones who'd stolen it in the first place."

"So we've got two completely different crimes to solve," Mallory said.

"Yes," Jupiter said. "And although we'll certainly try to find out who took the portfolio and recover what was taken from it, at the moment I think you'll agree that takes a very big back seat to trying to find Adam."

"You can say that again," Pete said.

"However," Jupiter added, "I don't think we should totally abandon the theft of the poems. It's entirely possible that it and the kidnapping are linked. Perhaps the kidnappers somehow learned about the French collector and his offer to buy the poems for a lot of money."

"Maybe the collector himself is behind it," Pete said.

"I doubt it," Jupiter said. "Presumably he's a well-known man and a French citizen in good standing. I can't imagine he'd have anything directly to do with the kidnappers. Think of his exposure. No, it seems much more likely that the kidnappers heard about the offer and imagined that if they could get their hands on the poems, they could sell them to the collector themselves. As we have discovered, criminals are not always the most brilliant thinkers."

He sat back and crossed his arms on his chest. "All right, then," he said. "Who might have known about the French collector's offer to buy the poems?"

Bob had been listening and not talking very much, though he was following Jupiter closely. But now he spoke up.

"The only person I can think of," he said, "other than Jacob and Adam, is Jacob's friend at the Tri-Faith Center. Luckily I've got his name and contact information. I wrote it down."

He pulled out his notebook and checked his notes.

"Hakim Rahmani," he said. "Maybe tomorrow we should call him and find out who, if anyone, he consulted with or told about the French collector's offer. Then we can track them down and see where it leads."

"Another excellent idea, Bob," Jupiter said. "If Mr. Suleiman really told no one other than his friend about the offer, then the only possible way the kidnappers could have learned about how much the poems might be worth would have been from someone at the Center, or someone who talked to someone there."

"But I think someone should go to the Center and talk to Mr. Rahmani in person, not just call," Mallory said. "The conversation could be tricky and it'll need someone who's clever at knowing what questions to ask and how to extract information."

"Who should go?" Pete asked.

"I'm going to work on the kidnapping," Jupiter said, "and try to figure out why the car seems to have vanished. I'd like to have Bob with me to help with the X account and the responses we got. So Mallory and Pete, you should go to the Center."

"I get it," Pete said, grinning. "I'm going to be the muscle, and Mallory is going to do the talking."

"O.K., then," Jupiter said. "I think we have a plan."

That evening, Jupiter added, he would call Father Samuel and ask him to drive them up to Danville where the car had last been sighted. They'd begin their investigation there.

Before they left, Bob would check the X account to see if any more information had come in. Mr. Suleiman would stay close to the phone at home in Alameda in case the kidnappers got in touch. And Mallory and Pete would call Andie and ask her to drive them to the Tri-

Faith Center in Oakland. There, Mallory would interview Mr. Rahmani.

They cleaned up in the kitchen and then made their way to their room. Bob was so tired he said very little, but then no one was talking much.

He lay down on his bed against the wall and stared up at the ceiling. Here he was, in a strange place, but surrounded by the people he knew best in the world. He couldn't help but think of Adam Suleiman. He was in a strange place, too, but isolated from everything he knew, his only company two men who could be treating him well or badly. Bob didn't know, but he feared it might be badly.

He remembered Adam's face when Jupiter had given him one of The Three Investigators business cards, and how it had shone with confidence in their ability. Bob took a deep breath. He hoped they could live up to the faith Adam had in them.

It felt strange to know that that faith had come about as a result of Bob's case reports — that Adam had been so drawn to the stories, or the style in which he had told them, that he'd come to feel as if Bob and Pete and Jupiter and Mallory were people he already knew, in real life.

Now he *did* know them – or he *had*, Bob thought grimly – and although neither he nor they could have imagined that they would be torn apart like this after a single meeting, Bob could only hope that they would soon be reunited.

11

Suspects!

Ever since Mallory had talked with Jacob Suleiman the day before, she'd been thinking, on and off, about her design for HQ2. Though she'd hoped to discuss architecture with him, there'd been no way to do that the first time they'd met, and since the second time had been just hours after Mr. Suleiman's son had been kidnapped, she would never in a million years have expected to talk about it then.

She'd joined him as he was looking at pictures of Adam as a boy, hoping she could console him. But at a time when most people would have given in to raw emotion, he instead had turned the talk to Mallory's designs for HQ2. Mallory knew that this must have been partly to distract himself from the situation he was in, but she also sensed that it was because Jacob Suleiman was so intensely − well, intensely *civilized*.

He'd remembered that he'd told her he hoped they'd have a chance to discuss her plans, and when he found himself with nothing else to do − at least nothing that would directly help Adam! – he'd asked her about them. By the end of their discussion, Mallory had felt confident that it *would* be possible to put a gorgeous new roof on her favorite Salvage Yard shed. She'd also told Mr. Suleiman that he'd make a great teacher.

He would, too, she thought – because the most interesting part of their conversation hadn't been about Headquarters at all. It had been about the thoughts she'd had after she'd seen the Land's End labyrinth. At the time, she hadn't articulated them to herself, but when she was talking to Adam's father, she'd been able to. She'd said she loved symmetry and order, and when the labyrinth at Land's End had given the illusion of order while violating it, it had suddenly occurred to her that what made a great city work was mostly its architecture.

In a pretty stumbling fashion, she'd talked about how great buildings made you feel solid and grounded – how intimately they connected you to the people who'd designed them, and the people who'd built them – and how disorienting it was to see a city like San Francisco falling into disarray.

When she'd tried to explain her thought that a well-ordered city – like Edinburgh, maybe – was reassuring even to people who didn't like cities much, but that San Francisco, as it was now, was surely unnerving even to people who *did* like them, Mr. Suleiman had seemed quite impressed. Though, he'd added, different cultures had different tolerances for daily disorder – and in Arab cities like Marrakesh or Tangier, the tolerance was generally higher than it was in the West!

All this had left Mallory feeling both flattered and even more worried about Adam. She could hardly imagine what it would do to the father if something bad were to happen to his son. He'd put his life back together after the death of his wife. But if he were to lose Adam –

Right now, as she and Pete waited for Andie to arrive to take them to the Tri-Faith Center, Bob and Jupiter were hunched over Bob's laptop, reviewing the latest information that had come in on X. All of a sudden Bob called out, "We just got an e-mail from Sarah Willoughby."

Mallory turned around, suddenly excited. "What did she say?" she asked.

"She found the letter I pinned to the door of her houseboat," Bob said. "She's happy to meet with us, but she doesn't know any family history that might help us figure out what had been hidden in the portfolio. But she was very interested to hear about the secret pocket. After she found my letter, she heard about Adam. She says that if we're friends of the Suleimans, we have a lot more on our minds right now than meeting with her. She wrote that she sometimes goes days without checking her e-mail. But she gave us her cell-phone number, if we want to call."

"I think we should call her right now," Mallory said. "After all, we know something she doesn't – that Adam's kidnappers have now asked for the portfolio of poems as a ransom. We don't have to actually *meet* with her to see if she knows anything that could help. People sometimes know things they don't know they know."

"I agree," Jupiter said. "But I'm afraid a phone call is going to have to wait until later today. Bob, why don't you forward Sarah Willoughby's e-mail on to Mallory? If she has time to call her after the meeting at the Tri-Faith Center she can do it then. You'll have seen the pots she threw for the Center by that time," Jupiter added to Mallory, "and they may give you a starting point for your conversation. People always like it when you can pay them sincere compliments to start off."

"That's a great idea," Mallory said. Bob

forwarded Sarah Willoughby's e-mail, and it had just landed in Mallory's Inbox when Pete called out.

"Andie's here," he yelled. "Time to go!"

Mallory stuffed her computer into her backpack and ran to meet Pete at the door.

"I think the demonstrations are finally calming down," Andie said when they had climbed into her taxi. "It'll make driving a lot easier. Last night the police finally made a bunch of arrests. They charged some people with disorderly conduct, trespassing, resisting a police officer, stuff like that. And they're actually keeping the people they arrested in jail this time. At least for a day or two. At least that's what I heard."

"That should slow them down," Pete said.

"I hope so," Andie said – and then they were off again. When they got to the Tri-Faith Center, Mallory really liked it. There were Moorish arches and Gothic spires, a tower that seemed both minaret and steeple, and on the floor in the entrance hall a series of mosaics that signs indicated were copies of mosaics in the floors of old European synagogues.

She and Pete stopped at the Reception Desk where an older woman peered at them kindly.

"We're trying to find Mr. Rahmani," Mallory said. "I called earlier and was told he'd be in today. We made an appointment."

The woman directed them down a hallway to an office where a brass plaque on the door said Hakim Rahmani, Research. No sooner had Mallory knocked than a voice invited them in.

Mr. Rahmani had an expectant air, as though he never knew what would happen when someone entered his office. He looked like a scholar to Mallory, thoughtful and alert, with gold-rimmed glasses and curly carefully cropped hair. Like Mr. Suleiman he had a small goatee, though his skin was a shade darker. Mallory was struck by the intelligence in his almond eyes.

"Hello," she said. "This is Pete Crenshaw, and I'm Mallory MacLeod."

"Welcome," Mr. Rahmani said, shaking their hands. "What can I do for you?"

Mallory had been worried that it might be hard to get information from Mr. Rahmani, but now that she'd met him, she was sure he'd be happy to tell them everything he knew. She'd thought she might have to draw on her acting skills, but there was clearly no need to be deceptive or to use subterfuge. It would simply be a matter of asking the right questions in the right order.

"We're here at the suggestion of Mr. Jacob Suleiman," Mallory said. Mr. Rahmani's face clouded, and when Pete told him they were friends of Adam's, he became visibly upset.

"Terrible," he said. "I'm sorry we are meeting under the shadow of these awful events. Please sit down." He himself settled behind his desk, which was a sea of papers, and he gestured toward two easy chairs in front of it.

"So you know everything that's happened?" Mallory asked as she sat down.

"Yes, indeed," Mr. Rahmani said. "It's in all the papers and on the television. I spoke with Jacob earlier today. He told me what the ransom demand is." He shook his head as if he couldn't believe it.

"We were with Mr. Suleiman last night," Mallory said, "and our friend Jupiter suggested to him that perhaps the kidnapping is connected to that French collector's offer to buy the poems."

Mr. Rahmani looked surprised. "I see," he said.

"And since you're the only person Mr. Suleiman told – "

"Ah!" Mr. Rahmani said. In a flash he understood everything. "So the only way the kidnappers could have learned that someone would pay a good deal of money for the poems is through me. That's a very disquieting thought, but let me see if I can remember who I talked to after Jacob called me to tell me about the offer he'd received."

He pushed his glasses higher on his nose, grabbed a pad of paper, and picked up a pencil. His eyes narrowed, he pressed his lips together, and he started making a list.

"Who did I talk to and when?" he said. "As I remember – " He looked very serious and intent. "It was just before lunchtime when Jacob called me, and after I hung up, I went to the cafeteria as I always do. I ran into Lucía Pérez, the Center's wonderful cook. She came here from Mexico and she's a fervent Catholic.

"I'd told her weeks before about the poems, and that the Center was going to receive them as a gift. She'd been so excited that I thought she'd be interested to hear that someone back in France was willing to pay a huge fortune for the poems. But I told her not to worry – they would still come to us, though we'd have to jump through some minor hoops to get them."

"Did you mention the matter to anyone else?" Mallory asked.

"I thought I needed to tell the Director, Philip Kendall, and the Center's lawyer, Melissa Liebowitz," Mr. Rahmani said, "so after lunch I dropped round their offices. I believe I mentioned it to both their secretaries as well."

He stared off past Pete and Mallory, checking his memory. "Yes, I'm sure. Those are the only ones, those four. I think they're all here today. Would you like to speak with them?"

When Mallory said yes, Mr. Rahmani picked up his phone and made a number of quick calls. "They're all here," he said. "They'll be expecting you."

Mallory and Pete thanked him for his help, and he offered to escort them to the lawyer's office. "We'll just take this shortcut across the courtyard," he said.

It was hot outside, after the Center's air conditioning, but Mallory thought the courtyard was beautiful – and not unlike the courtyard in Jacob Suleiman's own house. The ground underfoot was cobbled with gray stone;

there were various groups of dark wooden tables and chairs, all with colorful umbrellas to provide shade; and in odd arrangements around the courtyard Mallory saw gigantic terra cotta pots, with intricately braided rims, on which were inscribed religious symbols from the Islamic, Jewish, and Christian religions. They held carefully pruned and sculpted trees and shrubs – and although Mallory was sure these *must* be the pots Sarah Willoughby had designed and thrown, she asked Mr. Rahmani, just to be sure.

"Yes, those *are* Sarah's work," he said. "She's a good person as well as a good potter. Though she has an odd roommate. Or boat-mate, I should say! I can't remember his name, now, but he helped her deliver the pots, and I thought he had shifty eyes."

He laughed as if he didn't actually know what he meant by this – though it seemed to Mallory that he did. He nodded graciously, smiled, and left.

Melissa Liebowitz's secretary was a young man in his late 20s, with a bristle of blond hair and a large Adam's apple. His name plate identified him as Timothy Wessig. When Mallory explained why they were there, and asked if he might have mentioned the French collector's offer to anyone, he shook his head firmly.

"Absolutely not," he said. "Who would I have told, and why?" He seemed irritated by the suggestion.

"Because it's a good story?" Pete asked.

"No, no," Tim Wessig said. "I leave my work at the office."

Well, Mallory thought, he was so definite, she was sure he was telling the truth. There was nothing there.

His boss Melissa Liebowitz wore a navy blue pants suit and a white collared shirt open at the neck. She was in her early fifties, Mallory supposed. She shook her head firmly and spoke as if telling a secret. She was sure that she'd mentioned the monetary offer to no one, not even her husband. She pointed them down the hall to the director's office.

Philip Kendall's secretary was a middle-aged woman who looked like she spent quite a lot on her wardrobe. She wore pearl earrings and a gold choker. Her hair had been pulled back quite severely, and only her lips moved as she told Mallory and Pete that it was unthinkable that she had told anyone, anyone at all, about the Center's business. She looked as though the very question was an affront to her dignity. She pressed her intercom button and said, "Dr. Kendall? There are two young people here to see you."

"Send them in, will you, Dottie?" a voice said.

Philip Kendall was in his sixties, Mallory supposed, and the polar opposite of his secretary. He looked rumpled and tired. He had dark circles under his eyes and he appeared a bit bent over when he stood to shake their hands. His office was quite large and a bit messy, Mallory noted, and his wall was covered with awards and commemorations and citations he'd received during his career.

"Ghastly business," he said to them, "about young Suleiman. But the police are very good at this sort of thing, you know. I wouldn't worry."

"We're not worried," Mallory said – though she was lying. "We're just trying to figure out who could have taken him. After Mr. Rahmani told you about the offer the French collector made for the poems, did you mention it to anyone else?"

"Hmm," Kendall said. "Let's see. I was amazed, of course. An astonishing figure. I'd had no idea that the poems might be worth that much. I'm pretty sure I didn't mention it to anyone at the Center, but I may have mentioned it to my wife that evening. Let me think."

He squeezed his eyes shut as though that would allow him to visualize the conversation. He opened them again and looked a bit mournful. "Yes," he said. "I think I did mention it to Maureen. But I can't imagine she would have told anyone."

"Would you mind calling her and asking her?" Mallory said. "It's important."

Kendall smiled indulgently and picked up the phone. A few minutes later he hung up and turned to Mallory, a bit chastened.

"Yes, actually," he said. "She's a member of the choir at Grace Cathedral, where the poems were found after they were stolen, and she says she mentioned the money to two or three of the altos."

Oh, no, Mallory thought. If two or three choir members knew, the whole world could have known about it by the time the kidnapping occurred. She and Pete thanked Mr. Kendall for his time and help, and the two of them stood up to leave.

"Boy, that's not good news, is it?" Pete said when they were back in the hallway.

"Not really," said Mallory. "But I'm

thinking about what Mr. Rahmani said about Sarah Willoughby's roommate having shifty eyes. Who helped deliver her pots to the Tri-Faith Center and who we saw performing as a mime. Both Andie and Hiroka told us that he'd been arrested for being a con-artist. What if she told *him* about the Suleimans' poems and the portfolio? She could have told him about them after she read about them in the paper."

"That's true," said Pete. "But he also could have just read about them himself. Either way, the announcement in the paper didn't say anything about the French collector."

"That's true," Mallory said, feeling crestfallen. "I'm just so frustrated that we haven't accomplished anything yet that I'm grasping at straws. I guess I should call Andie."

"I think we should eat before we leave," said Pete. "Ever since Mr. Rahmani mentioned that wonderful cook, my stomach's been growling."

"So that's what that noise was," Mallory said, grinning. "I thought it was thunder. That's fine with me."

In the cafeteria, Mallory got a salad, but Pete started talking to a short woman with a friendly face who stood behind the steam table and looked to Mallory as if she'd come from Central America.

"Hola," Pete said. "Habla español?"

"Sí," the woman said, grinning. "Solamente." She looked very happy that someone had spoken to her.

"Bueno!" Pete said and began talking animatedly.

Mallory took her tray and found a small table. She shook her head. Pete was utterly irrepressible.

She watched as he and the woman kept talking. She couldn't believe how long the conversation was lasting. What could they be discussing? Food? Finally Pete grabbed his tray, and joined Mallory at her table.

"What was that all about?" Mallory asked.

Pete took a big bite of a chicken enchilada. "Well," he began when he'd finished chewing, "that wasn't Lucía Pérez, who Mr. Rahmani mentioned to us. But ever since I heard about her, I wondered if she might have told the story to someone else working in the kitchen with her. There's a lot of time to pass when you're chopping and stirring and tasting.

"So I asked Señora Molina – that's the woman I was talking to – if the cook had said anything about the poems. Sí, sí, she told me. She said Mrs. Pérez told her all about her conversation with Mr. Rahmani, and she couldn't believe someone would pay that much for a poem."

"Oh, no," Mallory said. "The list of suspects keeps multiplying."

"Wait!" Pete said. "So I asked her if *she* had told anyone, and she assured me, no, she hadn't told a soul, *no le dije a nadie.* But she couldn't vouch for the cook, who might have told other people, and Mrs. Pérez isn't here today."

"Great," Mallory said dispiritedly.

But Pete wasn't done.

"Then it occurred to me to ask Señora Molina if anyone else had been in the kitchen and might have heard the conversation," he said. "At first she said it was just the two of them, and then she said, wait a minute. Three times a week the Center gets a produce delivery in a big box truck, and the delivery guy carries the boxes into the kitchen and puts them right into the cooler.

"She said the delivery guy was there that day and might have overheard the conversation. She doesn't know his name – he's not very friendly, she said – or even the name of his company, but she thought he might be Chinese. He has a scar on his face, she said. When I asked if I could go back and look at the boxes, she told me no one was allowed but the people who worked in the kitchen."

As Pete was talking, Mallory was getting more and more intense and interested. Pete had been on the case the whole time, and that was a real investigation he'd just conducted. And she'd thought he was simply hungry!

"That is great work, Pete. I'm really impressed," she said.

"Fwanks," he said, his mouth full of refried beans.

"But now that we know this much," Mallory said, "Jupiter's going to want us to come back with more solid information about the delivery truck. Do you think Mrs. Molina would go look at the boxes and tell you the name of the company?"

Pete slapped himself on the side of the head. "Why didn't I think of that?" he said. He bounded from his chair and headed for the steam table. While he was gone, Mallory took a bite of his enchilada. Very good! she thought.

When Pete came back, he didn't seem to see that some of his food was missing.

"Got it!" he said. "It's called California

Bounty. She copied it down for me." He showed her the scrap of paper with the name written in pencil. "The boxes have these real colorful labels on them, she said — pictures of fruits and vegetables with a big black border all around."

What Pete said reminded Mallory of something, and as she thought back over the last few days, she remembered Seong's Grocery in Sausalito. Hadn't the crates of fruits and vegetables had stickers on them just like the ones that Pete had described? Mallory hadn't looked at them directly, but she'd seen them out of the corner of her eye.

California Bounty. The produce business that sold to Mrs. Seong also sold to the Tri-Faith Center. And then she remembered that when they'd been standing at the counter to pay, the first time they were in her store, Mrs. Seong had gone on and on about the company, and how they were also selling at farmers' markets all over the Bay Area. Walnut Grove and Concord.

And Danville.

A thrill ran up Mallory's spine. That meant that the delivery guy who brought produce to the Tri-Faith Center three times a week, and who probably overheard the cook and Mrs. Molina talking about the French collector and the huge sum of money he was willing to pay for the poems, also went to the farmers' market in Danville – where the trail of the kidnappers' car had gone cold.

But then she remembered that Mrs. Seong had said there was a whole fleet of trucks that California Bounty operated. "Many trucks, and they bring all over," she had said. So the connection between the Tri-Faith Center and the Danville Farmers' Market was tenuous at best.

Still, it was a lead – not the strongest that Mallory had ever encountered, but not nothing, either. She and Pete deposited their trays and started walking out toward the parking lot where Mallory called Andie. Since it would take her a while to get there, maybe now would be a good time to call Sarah Willoughby, she thought. She and Pete settled down in the shade where she opened her computer to get Willoughby's cell phone number. She hoped that by now Bob and Jupiter were up in Danville!

12

A Breakthrough At The Farmer's Market

Earlier that morning – in fact, as soon as Mallory and Pete were out the door and on their way to interview Mr. Rahmani – Jupiter had gone back to plotting the kidnappers' route on the map they'd started constructing at the Suleimans.

Bob read the new replies to their post on X and Jupiter added red dots that corresponded to sightings of the junker. Pleased as Jupiter was that Sarah Willoughby had answered their letter, he was totally engrossed in the task at hand. Almost all the new information confirmed that the car had traveled up through Orinda and Lafayette and then down the 680 freeway toward Danville.

Where it had disappeared.

It was a frustrating puzzle and one Jupiter couldn't solve, until Bob said, "Whoa! We just got a DM. Wait 'til you hear this!"

"A DM?" Jupiter asked.

"A Direct Message," Bob said. "Directly to us. Very useful since there aren't any restrictions on its length."

It was from Ricardo Juarez, an amateur ornithologist who lived in Danville. He'd been out and about the previous afternoon, observing a pair of yellow-rumped warblers who, he said, should have migrated into the high Sierra months before. But there they were, and Ricardo – with his camera and binoculars – had been excitedly observing and documenting the birds along a quiet and lightly traveled road outside Danville when the junker had suddenly appeared.

No doubt about it – he remembered the rusty orange door and the smiley face with the red tongue on the trunk. Being on the hill above the road, he'd seen it clearly. He hadn't taken a picture of it – he'd been too busy photographing the warblers and a dark-eyed junco he'd seen feeding on the ground. But he'd watched it slow down and stop behind a big truck.

Ricardo said that the back of the truck was open, with its ramp down. The truck had been there for a while, blocking the right-hand lane. He'd assumed it had engine trouble or a flat. He hadn't thought much about it at the time, but now, as he remembered, he'd looked down from the bushes he was hiding behind –

no one could have seen him if the warblers couldn't – and the car was gone. He was sure he'd have seen it if it had passed the truck and moved on, or if it had turned around and gone back the way it had come. Though his mind had been entirely on his birds, he remembered thinking, even at the time, that it was as if –

When he looked again, the ramp had been taken up and the back of the truck was closed. It was peculiar, but he was so excited about the yellow-rumped warblers that he'd never have thought of it again if he hadn't seen the picture of the car on X. Was it possible, he wondered, that the car had driven up *into* the truck and then the truck had driven away with the car in it?

That morning he'd gone out to where he'd seen the truck and car and taken a picture of the location in case The Three Investigators wanted to check it out for themselves.

"It's on Winding Creek Road," he wrote, "about four miles from where it leaves the highway. I marked the spot with a small pile of stones. Right near a big live oak."

Jupiter's mind was humming. He pinched his bottom lip. "That would explain it," he said. "Quite nicely. There were no more sightings of the car because it had, essentially, disappeared.

Ricardo's suggestion seems not only possible but likely. I think I once read a story or heard of a story in which something similar happened. Does it ring a bell with you?"

"Actually," Bob said, "it does. I can't remember the name of the story, but I remember thinking how clever it was. I think I should send a note to this guy to thank him."

Bob wrote a quick note and sent it off – and immediately afterwards, Father Samuel bustled through the door of the Golden Gate Hostel. They'd been expecting him, but even so, his appearance took Jupiter by surprise. He looked quite frazzled, as if he hadn't gotten much sleep the night before.

"Hello Bob, hello Jupiter," he said.

"Father Samuel," Jupiter said, rising. "Is there any news?"

The priest shook his head grimly. "A bunch of reporters were camped out in front of the house this morning, but Jacob hasn't heard a word. Nothing from the police."

"Sometimes no news is good news," Bob said, trying to be cheerful. "Anyway, *we* might have found something."

The priest looked hopeful and listened carefully as Bob told him about the message from Ricardo.

"But that's terrible!" the priest said. "How can we follow the car if it's inside another vehicle?"

"We can't," Jupiter said. "But maybe we can follow the second vehicle. We'll know more when we get to Danville."

"Then should we get going?" the priest asked.

"Definitely," Jupiter said.

As they once more traveled over the Golden Gate Bridge, through San Francisco, and over the Bay Bridge, Jupiter wondered how people could bear to live in places as crowded with people and roadways as this. It took forever to get anywhere.

"Where are Mallory and Pete today?" Father Samuel asked as they left Oakland and headed north toward Orinda.

"We just passed them," Jupiter said. "They're in Oakland at the Tri-Faith Center, talking to Mr. Suleiman's friend Mr. Rahmani. We have a theory that the kidnappers knew about the money the French collector was willing to pay for de Boissy's poems, so we're trying to track down everyone who might have heard about the offer. Mr. Rahmani is the only person Mr. Suleiman told, so we want to find out who Mr. Rahmani might have told."

Father Samuel sighed and looked very upset and unhappy.

"What's the matter?" Jupiter asked him.

"I feel responsible," the priest said.

"You said that yesterday, too," said Jupiter. "Did you also know about the offer?"

Father Samuel nodded glumly. "Adam told me. Even before it was in the papers. He and I have gotten very close since he became a believer."

"And did you tell anyone?" Jupiter asked.

The priest shook his head. "No, of course not," he said. "But I still feel – "

He sighed again, and it was clear that he had stopped talking for the time being.

That was all right with Jupiter. When the priest got talking, it could be hard to stop him, and at the moment Jupiter was happy to be left alone with his own thoughts. Right now, he was thinking again about religion having been more of a linchpin in the history of civilization than he had previously realized. It was certainly true that as religious belief had diminished, Western cultures seemed to be losing their confidence in their own values. You could see that and feel it all across San Francisco – and although Rocky Beach was still the town it had been ever since Jupiter could remember, some of the towns around it had been changing.

He turned his thoughts to Father Samuel. Ever since he had met the priest, Jupiter had had the sense that the priest knew more than he was telling about the theft and return of the portfolio – and now he was trying to decide exactly why he felt that. It might be partly the long-winded way in which Father Samuel told stories – but if that were the case, then his hunch was probably worthless. What else could it be, though? Jupiter wondered.

As Father Samuel turned off Highway 24 onto Winding Creak Road, Jupiter took a good look at the van's odometer. When they started approaching the four-mile mark, Jupiter asked the priest to go very slowly.

"We're looking for a pile of stones on the shoulder, and a large live oak," he said.

"There!" Bob said, pointing. Father Samuel pulled the van over and parked it. Jupiter saw that the stones had been carefully piled on top of one another. Though it was less than a foot high, it had obviously been arranged by human hands. Jupiter immediately began searching the shoulder and the road surface to see if there was anything unusual.

And there was – a scattering of what he was sure were vegetables pulped beneath the tires of a truck or car. He called Bob over.

"What does this suggest to you?" Jupiter asked.

Bob looked puzzled. "Is that an eggplant?" he asked.

"Half of one," Jupiter said. "There's also part of a zucchini, and three green beans."

"Well," Bob said. "I suppose they could have come from the truck."

Jupiter nodded. "My thought exactly. So maybe the truck carried produce. And look at this." He pointed to a nearby pothole that was almost full of water.

"That's strange," Bob said. "It hasn't rained around here in at least five months."

"What if it's melted ice?" Jupiter said. "To keep the produce chilled. What if they had to take everything the truck usually carried out in order to fit in the car, and what was left was a chunk of ice and this – " He pointed again at the vegetables.

"That's a great hypothesis, Jupiter," Bob said. "Let's search the area to see if we can find anything else."

While Bob explored to the left of the road, Jupiter ventured to the right. He passed the live oak and came to a large eucalyptus a little further off. Its bark was mottled and strips of it were hanging off. But on a darker section of the trunk Jupiter noticed something white. He looked closer. To his immense satisfaction, he saw three question marks carefully drawn with chalk. Adam had definitely been here!

He ran back to the van and told Bob and Father Samuel what he'd found.

"Remember how Adam specifically mentioned the chalk?" Jupiter asked Bob.

"Absolutely," Bob said.

"But why would the kidnappers have allowed Adam to wander in the woods?" Father Samuel asked.

"He probably told them he had to go," Jupiter said, "and they were busy getting the car into the truck, so they just said be quick about it. My guess is that he was actually looking for a way to leave us a clue. But where he got the chalk is anyone's guess. Nevertheless, he knew what to do with it once he got it. We ought to keep our eyes open. If he left one set of question marks, there are probably more!"

When they clambered back into the van, Jupiter said he thought they should drive on to Danville and find a place from which to call Mallory; the cell signal here was very weak.

Still, on the way, Bob tried and the call went through.

"I got Mallory!" Bob said. "I'm turning up the volume." He held the phone in the air between them. Mallory's voice was faint, but Jupiter could hear her.

"Bob!" Mallory said. "Are you in Danville yet?"

"Almost," Bob said. "Where are you?"

"Pete and I are with Andie," Mallory said. "And listen to this! Pete managed to find out that a produce delivery guy who works for a company called California Bounty – an Asian guy with a scar on his face – almost certainly overheard a conversation about the amount of money the French collector was willing to pay for the poems. And that's not all. I just called Sarah Willoughby and managed to learn that Joey Barton, her roommate – the mime we saw in the park – is friends with a guy she thinks drives a truck for California Bounty. A Chinese-American named David Wang."

Jupiter frowned. The name rang a distant bell.

"Also, she told me that Joey Barton had just called to say he'd been arrested and was in jail for supposedly being part of the demonstrations in Sausalito. He was driving through downtown, very late, and the police stopped him and saw he was dressed all in black and jumped to the wrong conclusion. Anyway, the main point is that he's a friend of this guy who drives for California Bounty!"

"I remember seeing some California Bounty crates at Seong's Market," Bob said excitedly. "And the prices on the boxes were written in white chalk. That's great news – and we've had a breakthrough, too!"

Quickly he told Mallory about the Direct Message they'd gotten from Ricardo Juarez.

"So we followed his directions," Bob said, "and we found the place where the truck was stopped on the road. Jupiter found some squashed produce. Not only that, he found three question marks chalked on the back of a tree. Adam must have drawn them!"

"Yes," Jupiter said. "If that grocery delivery guy works for California Bounty, our search has been vastly narrowed."

"I just looked up the company online," Mallory said. "They have a fleet of thirty white trucks with California Bounty painted on the sides – right over the painting of a large crate filled with oversized fruits and vegetables. They're very distinctive. They go to all the farmers' markets in the area including three around Danville. It turns out that Danville is pretty big – about 45,000 people. The Danville markets are held on Fridays and Saturdays."

"Then we're in luck," Bob said, "since it's Friday."

Jupiter was very pleased with how quickly and efficiently Mallory had thought through and conducted the research.

"Could you text Bob the locations of the three markets?" he asked.

"Sure," Mallory said. "Right away. Good luck!"

Bob hung up and Jupiter sat back in his seat. "This case is coming together much more efficiently than I could have hoped," he said.

Bob's phone buzzed and he flipped it open.

"Mallory's text just came in," he said. "She sure was quick." He gave Father Samuel the address of the first market — at Hap Magee Ranch Park, off Danville Boulevard, on the north side of Danville.

Jupiter pinched his bottom lip, wondering what they'd find. He was surprised when Bob's phone rang. It's Mallory again, he thought. She must have forgotten something.

But it wasn't Mallory.

"Mr. Suleiman!" Bob said. "Hello! You'd better talk to Jupiter." He handed the phone to the front seat. Though Father Samuel kept driving, he looked comprehensively alarmed.

Jacob Suleiman was very upset. "The police just called," he said. "They found the car at the bottom of an overlook in Bollinger Canyon, not far from Danville. It's smashed to pieces and there was a fire."

"Just the car?" Jupiter asked.

"Yes," Mr. Suleiman said. "No one was in it."

"That's certainly good news," Jupiter said.

"The police discovered it had been stolen a week before. They believe the car was parked at the overlook and then, when no one was around, it rolled off," Mr. Suleiman said.

"I'm sure the plan always was to destroy the car." Jupiter responded. "It was so visible, after all – just a decoy. But Bob and I have a very good idea about the vehicle the kidnappers are using now. I can't really explain it all to you at the moment, but please, don't worry. We're making good progress."

"That's fantastically good news," Mr. Suleiman said. He hung up.

As Father Samuel continued to head for the first market on the list, Jupiter said, "You mentioned earlier that it was Adam who told you about the offer the French collector had made."

The priest nodded. "In a way, Adam and I are better friends than Jacob and I are these days – though I've known Jacob far longer. I think that's because Adam and I share a faith in God, and Jacob doesn't. Also, Adam and I are very interested in Jacques de Boissy's work, and in these particular poems."

"Oh, yes?" Jupiter said.

The priest smiled. He seemed different somehow – as if a burden had been lifted from him. Jupiter could only suppose it was due to the fact that they now seemed close to rescuing Adam.

"Of course," he said expansively, even a bit boastfully, "I've known about the poems a great deal longer than Adam has. I first found them in the Suleimans' library, years before Adam was even born."

This was new information to Jupiter, and very interesting. "Go on," he said, encouraging the priest.

"When I was in Morocco all those years ago," Father Samuel said, "I got to know the Suleiman family when Jacob was still quite young. Still a boy. Jacob's father gave me access to his library. It was full of wonderful old books and manuscripts, and I browsed it thoroughly. One day I came across this odd leather portfolio and I took it down off the shelf and carried it to one of the reading tables. That was the first time I ever read the villanelles. Of course I loved them immediately – who would not? – and I could tell right away from his fervency and humility that Jacques de Boissy could never have lost his faith in God."

"He lost his faith in God?" Bob asked.

It was as though the priest hadn't realized what he was saying. He shook his head vehemently. "It was a rumor I ran across. That for some reason de Boissy's faith wavered. I never believed it. Never. Not for a moment." The priest had set his jaw and was staring straight ahead out the windshield at the highway he was speeding down.

Hmmm, Jupiter thought. The priest seemed quite adamant about de Boissy's faith, and about the poems as proof of that. Perhaps a bit too adamant.

As they drove into Hap Magee Ranch Park, they immediately saw a cluster of pickups, cars, and trucks, tables and small white tents, as well as the sign MARKET TODAY! Father Samuel said he'd stay with the van to give Bob and Jupiter more freedom. As soon as they got close to the market itself, Jupiter spied a large and very clearly marked California Bounty truck.

"Let's go!" Jupiter said. But the driver with the truck was a woman, very friendly, with curly red hair tied back by a blue bandana. They spoke to her briefly, but Jupiter felt almost sure she hadn't been involved in the kidnapping — and she certainly wasn't Asian. They thanked her and ran back to the van.

The second market was at a small park in downtown Danville, and it was mobbed. Aside from crates of ripe tomatoes, corn, squash, beans, arugula, peaches, figs, and garlic, there were tables where people were selling the breads and pastries they'd baked, the jams and cheeses and condiments they'd made. This time, the California Bounty truck was attended by an African-American man in his late thirties with four small children who stood behind the table on which he'd arranged his produce, all with bright expectant faces.

"Not him," Bob said, and Jupiter concurred.

On the far side of Danville, at Osage Station Park off El Capitan Road, they found the last market. It lacked the energy and bustle of the first two and had the fewest stalls. The vendors sat in folding chairs under their pop-up canopies, searching the sparse crowd for potential customers.

After walking the length of the market, Jupiter and Bob found the California Bounty truck. Unfortunately, once again, the driver wasn't Chinese-American, but a good-looking young Mexican-American man – about thirty, Jupiter thought. He hadn't bothered to set up a table or unload his produce. He seemed jittery as he walked back and forth in front of the ramp, and when a woman holding an infant stopped, he urged her to walk up the ramp and into the truck itself.

"Great stuff," he said, "very fresh."

She shook her head and walked on.

When Jupiter and Bob approached him, he looked at them as if wondering whether they could actually produce a sale. "What have you got?" Jupiter asked.

"Go on up and see," the man said, gesturing toward the ramp.

The interior of the truck had deep shelves on both sides, all of them loaded with flimsy wooden crates holding fruits and vegetables. Jupiter let his eyes dart everywhere, looking for clues. All the way at the back, near the cab, he found one.

"Look at this!" he hissed at Bob. On the floor, almost hidden by one of the racks of vegetables, were three white question marks scrawled in chalk – and next to the question marks was a hastily drawn rendition of the labyrinth at Chartres. Not only that, but in the middle of the labyrinth, where the rose-petalled pattern should be, Adam had put his own initials, A.S.

"Wow!" Bob said. "Can you believe this? Adam is an amazingly smart guy. Imagine coming up with this under these conditions!"

"Keep your voice down," Jupiter said. "Of course all these racks would have had to be taken out in order for the car to drive in. But Adam was here, in this truck, all right. Take a picture of the chalk marks."

Bob used the camera on his cellphone as Jupiter chose four peaches. He bagged them and paid the man. While the vendor was talking to another customer, Bob managed to snap a picture of him and another of his license plate.

"Oh this is wonderful news!" Father Samuel said when they told him what they'd found. "We should wait for the market to end and then follow him!"

"I agree," said Jupiter. "We don't want

to lose this truck. Although the man who's driving it was probably not connected to the kidnapping, he seems pretty jittery. He may know something – and even if he doesn't, he may clean the interior of the truck and destroy the evidence. I suppose we should also call the police, but I don't want to spook this guy or let him know we're onto him."

"That's for sure," Bob said. "Though now that we have a photo of the license plate, maybe the best thing to do would be to get the police to find out who was driving the truck when the bird-watcher saw it on the road. They could stake out his house and follow him when he goes to feed Adam and make sure he's O.K. The kidnappers are probably holding Adam in a warehouse or basement somewhere."

Jupiter knew that Bob was probably right, but even so, he felt reluctant to involve the police just yet. He remembered the way they'd been at the Suleimans' house. In addition, he couldn't help but consider that the police had done nothing so far but find a burnt-up car – which Mr. Suleiman said had actually been handed to them when someone walking in the canyon reported it.

Meanwhile, The Three Investigators

seemed to have uncovered the identities of the two men who had probably kidnapped Adam – Joey Barton and David Wang.

In fact, there was a part of him – a big part – that felt frustrated at the prospect of having the police take over their last case of the summer. He'd hate for it to end like that – especially because they'd made no progress yet in finding out who had stolen the poems and then returned them. Or why.

But as Jupiter hesitated – torn between one action and the other – suddenly a very old and beaten-up motorcycle came roaring into the farmers' market and skidded to a stop beside the California Bounty truck. The man driving it was dressed entirely in leather and he wore a gigantic black helmet with a very dark visor. As he kicked down the kickstand and pulled his helmet off, Jupiter could see he was Chinese-American. Not only that, but he had a gigantic scar across his cheek!

Jupiter jumped out of the van to better see and hear what was going on. He was standing no more than fifteen feet away, and as he pretended to check the passenger side mirror, he saw the Mexican-American man he'd bought the peaches from running up to the new arrival.

"What took you so long?" he said. "I've got better things to do than take over your truck while you lounge around in your house. Just because we both use the same mechanic doesn't mean we're friends! Give me my bike!"

He handed the keys of the truck to the motorcycle driver, and as Jupiter climbed back into Father Samuel's van, the Mexican-American jumped onto the motorcycle and gunned it away from the parking lot. The Chinese-American closed the back of the California Bounty truck, tossed his helmet into the front seat, climbed in after it, and turned the engine on.

Sometimes events made your decisions for you, Jupiter reflected, as he abandoned all thoughts of calling the police.

He turned to Father Samuel.

"You'd better follow that truck," he said. "And step on it!"

13

Adam Leaves A Clue

As Father Samuel wove in and out of the sparse traffic headed toward Mount Diablo State Park, Bob felt both nervous and excited about being on the tail of the California Bounty truck. He was also more than a little annoyed that the chase was making it impossible for him to get on the Internet. He desperately wanted to check out the area in front of them to see where David Wang was headed.

In fact, enough was enough, Bob thought. The summer had started with an investigation in which he'd really wished he'd had a smartphone, and although at the time he'd been able to get what he needed by guessing the password to a protected Wi-Fi network, now it was even more crucial that he have access to a source of information – and without having to stop somewhere along the road.

Whatever else happened, by the time the next summer season started, he was going to have a smartphone. In the meantime, he stared out the window at the increasingly hilly landscape as Father Samuel drove toward Mount

Diablo, which rose in the distance to a barren peak, its lower slopes a combination of chaparral and wind-blown live oaks.

For some reason, Father Samuel thought this was a perfect time to discourse on the mountain's name. Bob had noticed before that the priest had an oddly rambling way of talking, but this really took the cake. Of course, Jupiter had started the ball rolling down what appeared to be an endless hill by saying that Mount Diablo was rather a spooky name.

To this random and essentially meaningless observation, Father Samuel had responded emphatically.

"Diabolical," he said unhappily. "Not just spooky. In fact, people have petitioned to have the name changed. In the early 19th century several members of the Chupcan tribe escaped from the Spanish near the mountain, supposedly guided by peculiar lights they saw." He paused, thought a moment. "Then the Chupcan won a battle against the Spanish in 1850, aided by a strange dancing figure the Spanish general called the devil. Other people have seen flickering lights where there were none, and there have been frequent sightings of black panthers!"

"I thought black panthers only lived in

southeast Asia," Jupiter said.

"Exactly!" the priest said.

Jupiter cleared his throat. "We need to remember that Adam was not taken by the devil, and that if he's somewhere around Mount Diablo, he's in a building we can discover."

"Or *could* discover," Bob said gloomily. "If we only had a smartphone."

Father Samuel looked surprised. "A smartphone? But we do! At least I do. At least, I think it's still there. The diocese gives all its priests one. I rarely use it myself, if I can avoid it, but the other day I plugged it in for a while. It's in the glove box."

"You're kidding," Bob said, completely forgetting what he'd learned about being polite. The glove box was right in front of him and he opened it now to find what appeared to be an almost-brand new Apple iPhone. He turned it on, but as he was about to ask Father Samuel what the passcode was, he saw that it had been set so as not to require one.

In a moment, he was looking to see if there was a David Wang in Danville, but when he found six in the town and the immediate area – with different middle names – he gave up.

"Too many possibilities," he said. "Let me try pulling up some aerial photos to see if there's anything that looks like a place they could have taken Adam."

As Father Samuel continued to follow the California Bounty truck, Bob found the aerial photos he wanted.

"Here's an abandoned shipping container," he said excitedly, "about two miles from the entrance to Mount Diablo State Park."

It was near the highway in a desolate stretch, stunted pines and boulders surrounding it. Bob suddenly felt sick at the thought that Adam might be held inside it. It was exactly the sort of place the kidnappers *would* be keeping him — someplace he couldn't get out of and where no one would hear him if he called out.

After more searching Bob found an old cabin, its windows boarded up, its porch caved in and part of the roof as well. It looked as if no one had been there in years — a derelict retreat and fire hazard, but a reasonable choice for some kidnappers looking for a place to secure their victim. If Father Samuel lost sight of the California Bounty truck, at least Bob had found some possible locations that he and Jupiter could check out.

Since there was more traffic on the road to Mount Diablo than Bob would have imagined, most of the time Father Samuel was able to keep another vehicle between them and the truck. It was the height of the camping season, and the cars on the road approaching the state park were actually going pretty slowly.

As Father Samuel gripped the steering wheel anxiously, Bob unbuckled his seat belt and scrambled between the bucket seats to join Jupiter in the bench-seat behind them. He wanted to talk to him privately about a strange thought he'd had ever since the leather-clad man had taken off the helmet and Bob had seen the serious scar that slashed his left cheek.

Bob had the funny feeling he'd seen that man − and that scar − before, but because he couldn't remember where, he'd been trying to convince himself he hadn't. After all, earlier in the summer, he'd actually been able to identify a villain by a tiny scar under his eye; maybe he just had scars on the brain somehow.

"Hey, Jupe," he said as he clicked on his new seat belt. "Maybe I've seen too many movies, but that scar looks incredibly familiar. The guy does too, actually. But I've rarely been to San Francisco, and I doubt he's been to Rocky Beach. I think I must be imagining things."

"Maybe not," Jupiter said. "When Mallory first mentioned his name, it sounded oddly familiar, and when he first pulled off that helmet, I had the feeling I'd seen him before, at a moment of tension or danger. Of course, that could easily have been because of the current circumstances, but I wish we had his middle name and could do a better search."

"Maybe we should call Mallory and get more details about what Sarah Willoughby told her," Bob said. "Or maybe we should just call Sarah Willoughby directly."

"Do it," said Jupiter. So Bob took out his own cellphone − into which he'd programmed Sarah Willoughby's number − and dialed her. She picked up right away, and when Bob had introduced himself and told her that Mallory had filled him in on the earlier call, he asked if she could remember anything else about David Wang.

"Did he have a middle name?" he asked. "Or a nickname, or anything like that?"

"He may have," Sarah Willoughby said. "But if so, I never heard it. Or if I heard it, I don't remember. The one thing I *do* remember that I didn't mention to Mallory is that apparently he originally lived in Auburn, but when he lost his job up there about a year ago, he moved to the Bay area."

"He's from Auburn?" Bob said intently. "Do you know what he did there?"

"I have no idea," Sarah said. "But it must have been something that made him a lot of money — a lot more money than driving a vegetable truck! Joey told me he was still really angry that he'd lost that job, where he was supposedly about to make a big score. That's what Joey said, anyway — that his friend had told him he was going to make a big score, but that some young jerks had come along and ruined everything."

"What had they ruined? Do you know?" asked Bob.

"I have no idea. I'm sorry," Sarah said.

"That's all right," said Bob. "You've been incredibly helpful anyway. We'll let you know when we find out something else ourselves."

He clicked his phone shut and started searching for David Wangs in Auburn.

This search went much better than the one in Danville had. There was only one David Wang in Auburn itself, and only two in the surrounding area. Plugging in the name and address he'd found for the David Wang in Auburn, he did a general search and found the man had worked for an Auburn real estate developer — and as Bob looked at the name of this developer, he felt hot, then cold, and then hot again.

"Look at this," he hissed, holding out the phone to Jupiter and pointing to what he'd found.

"Are you thinking what I'm thinking, Jupe?" he asked. "There could hardly be more than one John Chang Real Estate in the town of Auburn!"

Jupiter's eyes flashed. "We weren't wrong in our instincts," he said. "He was one of John Chang's henchmen! And the last time we saw him, he was running away from the Carnegie Library in Auburn. I can see his face very clearly against the wall of Connor O'Malley's studio."

"Yes," said Bob. "And *we* must have been the young jerks who came along and ruined everything when he was about to make a big score. John Chang must have promised him a cut of the money from Isabella's Chang's gold!"

He was going to go on and say more, but just then Father Samuel said, "Oh, no!" and Bob looked up to see that the California Bounty truck had darted off the main road leading to Mount Diablo – and that Father Samuel, stuck in a line of traffic and unable to respond as quickly he would have liked, had missed the turn.

"What should I do?" Father Samuel said in what sounded like despair.

"Find a place to turn around as quickly as possible, then go back and get on that other road," said Jupiter.

Father Samuel did what Jupiter had suggested, but because of both the traffic and the lack of other secondary roads, it took at least ten minutes for the van to get back to where the California Bounty truck had turned.

Although Father Samuel drove as fast as he safely could once he reached that road, there was clearly no chance they'd ever catch up with the truck now, and when he saw that, Father Samuel moaned.

"Oh, no," he said. "This is all my fault again."

As Bob was reflecting, with a fair degree of irritation, that Father Samuel seemed to like to take responsibility for things he really couldn't have helped, Jupiter surprised him by leaning forward and saying, "Losing the truck wasn't your fault. But I think what you're really concerned about is that Adam getting kidnapped may have been."

"What do you mean?" Father Samuel sputtered.

"You've said it was your fault twice," Jupiter said. "When Pete asked you why, you said that, you told him it was because you'd encouraged Jacob and Adam to give the poems to the Tri-Faith Center."

"That's right!" said Father Samuel. "And I had!"

"But then Mr. Suleiman said that Adam hadn't required any encouragement. So why do you still feel guilty about something that had nothing to do with you?" Jupiter asked.

From a lifetime's acquaintance with Jupiter Jones, Bob felt certain that Jupiter would never have asked Father Samuel this question unless he'd already hypothesized an answer — but just as Bob was about to say that, Father Samuel came around a corner of the road, and all three of them saw the California Bounty truck parked in the driveway of a small, shabby ranch house with a large metal shed standing back a little from the road.

It was a residential area that had seen better days. One house had a FOR SALE sign and looked as though no one lived there any more. The other houses were all single-story, with asphalt roofs and burned out lawns, and they looked like they'd been constructed from the same plan. The place had a singularly depressing feeling.

As they watched, a sleek souped-up motorcycle, driven by a man dressed all in leather, roared out of the ranch house's driveway and past them. His face was invisible; he was wearing an enormous black helmet with the visor once again pulled down.

"Bob, write down the license number," Jupiter said. And to Father Samuel, he added, "I think you should keep driving. Don't stop until you get around the next corner. Then turn around and park out of sight of the house."

Without asking any questions, Father Samuel did what Jupiter had asked, and soon the van was parked on the shoulder of the road, about three hundred yards from the house, but just out of sight of it.

Bob and Jupiter climbed down. "It would be good if you stayed here," Jupiter said to Father Samuel. "But take your phone back, and if we get into any trouble, call 911. Otherwise, just wait for us to get back to the van."

"I will," said Father Samuel. "Good luck."

As casually as possible, Bob and Jupiter

strolled along the shoulder of the road. No one was out in the yards. No children were playing. The whole place had a deserted feeling, and although two or three cars passed them, going one way or the other, no one seemed to think that the sight of two boys walking along a road on a summer afternoon was anything to wonder about.

Bob was glad of that, and even gladder when Jupiter said that he had a plan.

"I think we should just go up to the front door and knock," he explained. "If someone answers, we can say that we're bicyclists and that you hit a pothole and blew your tire. We'd like to use their phone to call our parents to come and pick us up. I've never had a cellphone, and yours is out of juice."

"Got it," Bob said, and soon they were standing on the small front stoop and knocking.

Luckily – at least Bob assumed it was luckily – no one came in answer to their knock, and after trying two or three more times, Jupiter said, "All right. We'll assume no one's home. Let's see if we can get into that metal shed."

Of course! thought Bob. If this David Wang guy actually lived here and had indeed been one of Adam's kidnappers, that shed was just the sort of place they might be keeping Adam. They hurried to the shady area under the trees where the shed was standing and banged on the metal. Both of them called out, "Adam? Are you in there? Adam, are you all right?" But no one answered, and the sliding metal doors at the front had been padlocked together in the middle.

"Let's see if there's a window at the back," Jupiter said.

Making their way to the rear of the shed, they found a man-door with a glass panel on the top covered with a pull-down shade. The padlock hanging on the doorjamb's hasp was unfastened, but when Jupiter tested the door-knob, he found it was locked.

"Oh, no," said Bob. "How are we going to see what's inside?"

"Like this," said Jupiter. He picked a stone up from the ground, smashed the glass in the window, and carefully reached inside to un-lock the door.

"If this guy turns out to be innocent, we can pay for the broken glass," Jupiter said.

He pushed the door open and stepped inside. It was dark and dusty. Just a few rays of sunlight filtered in through gaps in the metal. Bob strained to see until Jupiter hit the light switch beside the door.

The shed had a workbench with tools at the back, as well as a lot of cardboard boxes and miscellaneous junk, but there was also a blown-up air mattress with blankets and a pillow, a cup and a jug of water at its side.

Bob gulped. "Do you think that mattress and water were for Adam? And if so, where *is* he? He isn't here any more."

"No," said Jupiter. "But I bet he was. And, if he was, I bet he tried to leave us a sign like the one he left in the California Bounty truck."

Although Bob and Jupiter looked carefully at the walls and the ceiling and the workbenches and the floor, they couldn't find any question marks.

"Maybe he lost the chalk," Bob said.

"Maybe," said Jupiter. "But there are marking pens on the workbench, and if he'd actually been here, he could have used one of those. I don't know. I guess it's possible that the mattress and the water are here for some other reason. Maybe the guy has a dog who sleeps on a mattress in the shed."

"With a blanket and pillow?" Bob asked. Following an instinct, he leaned over, lifted the edge of the mattress and was thrilled to see three red question marks – and next to them another labyrinth with the initials A.S. in the middle.

"Look, Jupe," Bob said. "You were right. He used a marking pen. The same marks he drew in the truck! But what do you think that other mark is? The one next to it?"

Whatever it was, it had been drawn more hastily than the others, and to Bob, it looked a little like a jug or pot with an arrow pointing to it. Nearby, but far enough away so that Bob couldn't be sure if it had anything to do with the marks was the name Isaiah, followed by the numbers 64 and 8.

"Whatever it is, it's weird," he said.

"Take a picture of it," Jupiter said, "then let's get back to the van and decide what to do next."

Carefully, Bob took pictures of the three question marks, the labyrinth with Adam's initials in the middle, the pot with the arrow pointing to it, and the word Isaiah. Then he and Jupiter left the shed, carefully closing the door behind them.

Bob felt like running back to where Father Samuel was waiting, but Jupiter pointed out that if David Chang came back and saw them running away from his house, he would certainly be suspicious.

So the two of them walked back to the van as slowly as they had left it — though when Father Samuel saw them, he threw open the driver's side door and leapt out so quickly that anyone passing would have had to be curious.

Luckily, no one *was* passing, and soon they were all safely back in the van again, and Father Samuel was starting it and putting it on the road.

"Well?" he asked urgently. "What did you find?"

"We managed to get into the shed at the back of the property," Jupiter told him. "There was a mattress and a jug of water on the floor, and underneath the mattress, there were three question marks drawn with a red magic marker, and also the same labyrinth we found in the California Bounty truck — the labyrinth at Chartres, but with Adam's initials instead of a rose in the middle."

"Oh, praise God!" said Father Samuel. "That means that Adam is all right! And now that we know where they've been keeping him, we should surely call the police!"

"You're probably right," Jupiter said. "At the least, we should head back toward Alameda and tell Mr. Suleiman what we've discovered. The problem is, although Adam was certainly at David Wang's ranch house for a while, he isn't there now, and I bet he's been moved somewhere else. But where is that somewhere else and why was he moved to begin with? It's not that I don't trust the cops – but after all, the way they've been handling this kidnapping so far hasn't inspired confidence."

"That's true, Jupe," Bob said. "But the cops in Danville and the ones in Alameda aren't the same cops. Anyway, what we really need to find out is where David Wang was heading on his motorcycle. And since I got his license number, couldn't the police put out an all-points bulletin or something?"

"They probably could," Jupiter said, "though I really think we need to report to Mr. Suleiman and let him decide how he wants to handle this. He may have decided that the best and safest thing to do is to turn the poems over to the kidnappers – who for all we know, may have called him by now to arrange the transfer. If he *has* decided to do that, then calling the cops and having them track down David Wang's motorcycle might be a very bad thing to do. Wang and Barton can be picked up later."

"Oh, dear," said Father Samuel.

"Jupiter's right. If only we knew where Adam was now. Maybe he didn't know where he was being taken next himself, but he's so smart, so well-organized – and also so full of faith in God! – that if he knew where he was going, I can't imagine he wouldn't have found a way to tell us. Was there nothing else on the floor?"

"Just a thing that looked like a pot or a jug," said Bob. "With an arrow pointing to it. I thought maybe he was thirsty, and just doodling. That he hoped someone would come and fill the jug again soon. There was also the word Isaiah and some numbers, but to tell you the truth, I wasn't even sure that he had written that part of what was on the floor. Does he know someone named Isaiah?"

"You saw the word Isaiah and some numbers?" asked Father Samuel. "What were the numbers?"

"I can't remember," said Bob. "Just a minute." He pulled his cellphone out of his pocket and scrolled through the photographs he had taken in the shed until he found the numbers. "The first number was 64, and the second number was 8."

"It's a reference to a Bible verse," said Father Samuel, "Isaiah 64:8. And if I'm remembering it correctly, it reads: 'But now, O Lord,

You are our Father, We are the clay, and You our potter, And all of us are the work of Your hand.'" Adam must have been sitting in the shed thinking about the way God remade him when he first read the villanelles and then visited Grace Cathedral! What a wonderful boy he is — and so full of faith!"

"Maybe," said Jupiter tensely, "but when we were having breakfast with Mallory's friend Hiroka, Mrs. Ito told us that Sarah Willoughby has a studio with a kiln somewhere in the outskirts of Sausalito. What if the jug with the arrow pointing toward it was actually a pot Adam drew? I bet Adam was actually telling us where he was being taken next!"

14

Pete Drops In

Pete was sitting in the back of Andie's car as she pulled up to the Golden Gate Hostel about fifteen minutes later. When Mallory's phone rang, he sat forward eagerly, thinking it must be Bob calling with an update. But it was Sarah Willoughby again. Pete wondered what she wanted.

Mallory told her they'd just gotten back to the hostel in Sausalito. "I can't talk right now," Mallory said, "but I'll call you in a little while."

Mallory paid Andie as Pete got out of the car. He patted the driver's side door.

"Thanks a lot, Andie," he said. "You've been great. Maybe we'll see you again sometime. Or maybe you and Phoebe can come down to Rocky Beach when we have our Tall Ship Jubilee celebration!"

Andie drove away, he and Mallory climbed the steps to the hostel's porch, then made their way to their room.

Pete's mind was humming. He was still excited that his hunch about Lucía Pérez had

256

been right – she'd told Señora Molina all about the French collector's offer, and the Asian guy who worked for California Bounty had overheard them. Pete didn't have many hunches, and when he did, they often amounted to very little. But this time he'd gotten it right.

In short order Sarah Willoughby had told Mallory that the Asian guy was probably named David Wang, a friend of her roommate Joey. And then Jupiter and Bob had found the question marks Adam had left.

All of this gave Pete confidence that, before the day was over, Jupiter and Bob would be calling to say they'd tracked Adam down and that he'd soon be reunited with his father. Pete was really, really relieved, because he'd seen how worried Mr. Suleiman had been when they'd been at his house the day before.

The truth of the matter was, Pete couldn't stop thinking about how horrible it must be for Adam. Though Pete had been in some nasty situations of his own, he'd never actually been kidnapped, if that meant taken by someone and held for ransom – with the threat of death if the ransom wasn't paid. But he thought he knew how Adam felt. Ransom or not, Pete had been held captive against his will.

And it had been bad.

He'd never really thought of it before, but, in a way, being kidnapped was a lot like being made into a slave. He'd been thinking about slavery lately because the last time he'd worked on his history paper about Lieutenant Stephen Decatur, it had occurred to him that when Decatur had led his men on that really dicey maneuver to free the *Philadelphia*, he wasn't just risking being killed by the Barbary pirates – he was risking being captured by them and turned into a slave. This seemed to Pete even worse than being killed.

And when Andie's car had been surrounded by the mob of demonstrators, Pete had felt a kind of panic verging on suffocation. Later he'd talked with Jupiter about how trapped he'd felt, and Jupiter had agreed. There was nothing worse, Pete thought, than having your freedom stolen from you – and he really could hardly bear to think that it had now happened to Adam.

Just then, Mallory said, "What's going on, Pete? You look worried."

"I was thinking about Adam," Pete said, "and how it feels to be held somewhere against your will. Don't you think you should call Sarah Willoughby back?"

Mallory looked stricken. "Of course," she said, pulling out her phone and punching the number. "I was just so happy to be back here – and I was thinking about my plans for HQ2."

Pete watched her as the number rang, and then she snapped the phone shut. "It went straight to voice mail," Mallory said. "I wonder what she wanted."

Before she even had time to put the phone away, it rang again – and this time it was Bob.

Pete couldn't hear what Bob was saying. He leaned forward eagerly. Mallory was nodding. "Yes," she said, "we're back in Sausalito. At the hostel." Then the expression on her face changed to amazement and consternation. "You're kidding!" she said. "Really?"

"What?" Pete said. "What?"

"You think he's on his way there now?" Mallory asked. "But we don't have any way to get there. We'd have to call Andie again."

"Tell me!" Pete said, but she shook her head and held up her hand.

"What about the police?" she said. "Well, I guess we'll call her then." Pete was tense with excitement. When Mallory finally hung up, she turned to him.

"Remember John Chang?" she said. "The guy up in Auburn who was trying to find Li Chang's gold before we did? He had backup with him when he came to the Carnegie Library, and the guy had a big scar across his cheek. If you can believe it, his name was David Wang."

"You mean Sarah Willoughby's roommate's friend?" Pete asked incredulously.

Mallory nodded. "He was at one of the farmers' markets Bob and Jupiter just visited. With a California Bounty truck! Father Samuel followed the truck to Wang's house, but when they got there, he raced off on a motorbike. Jupiter and Bob checked out a metal shed on the property, and they found signs that Adam had been there.

"It's all speculation at this point," she added, "but Jupiter thinks that Wang may be headed for Sarah Willoughby's studio, here in Sausalito. Something about a Bible verse about people being clay and God being a potter. Since we're already here in Sausalito, Jupiter wants us to find the studio and see if Adam's there. Bob gave me Wang's license plate number. He's wearing black racing leathers and he has a black helmet on."

"What about the police?" Pete asked.

"Bob and Jupiter talked to Mr. Suleiman and he said he didn't want the police involved – that he was afraid they'd make the situation worse if they went in with guns blazing."

"But how are we going to get there?" Pete said, his voice rising. "And where is the studio?"

"Bob didn't know, but it shouldn't be hard to find since we know who owns it. First let me try Sarah Willoughby again. After that I'll call Andie."

As Mallory keyed in the number, Pete heard tires on gravel and peered out of the window to see an unfamiliar car – an old Subaru Forester. As he watched, a woman in her late 50s, her shoulder-length dark hair streaked with gray, got out and stared up at the hostel. She wore blue jeans and a smock, and she looked unhappy. Unhappy and anxious. She had long slender fingers and she wound them together in front of her waist.

All of a sudden, one of her hands dived into her jeans pocket and emerged holding a cellphone. Somehow it didn't surprise Pete when she started speaking into it just seconds before Mallory said, "Is that Sarah Willoughby?"

"I think she's standing in the driveway!"

Pete said. "Come on! Let's go meet her!" A minute later, he and Mallory had grabbed their gear and were running down the steps toward the Subaru.

"I'm Pete, and this is Mallory," Pete said, "and boy, are we glad to see you. Our friends Bob and Jupiter think the kidnappers may be holding Adam Suleiman in your studio! They want us to get out there! Can you take us?"

"Yes, of course," Sarah said. "Hop in!"

Pete was impressed by how quickly she got it together and started driving – especially because she was clearly bewildered by the news they'd just given her. Though not, it seemed to him, completely surprised. Once she was underway, she said, "They're keeping him in my studio? Was this Joey's idea? I'll kill him. Are they keeping him in the room with the kiln?"

"We don't know," Mallory said. "We're not even sure he's there. Why did you ask about the room with the kiln?"

"That's where *I'd* keep someone I didn't want to escape," Sarah said. "The room has no windows, but it has a bathroom off to one side. I padlock the door when I'm not there because I'm always afraid some kids will get into the house, turn the kiln on, and hurt themselves.

"The place wasn't built to be a studio," she added. "The guy who built it really loved the faraway views of the bay. There's a huge deck surrounding it – a bit like a ship's deck. The house itself is pretty small, just a single main room and a bedroom at the back. I took the windows out of the bedroom where the kiln is – and I use the main room to throw pots. It has good light – two skylights – and a lot of big windows and glass doors opening onto the deck."

As they reached the outskirts of Sausalito, Pete began tensing up. They were so close to finding Adam, and Pete was worried that something would go wrong. And, of course, it did.

Sarah stepped on the brakes and stared down the street where a group of black-clad figures had massed.

"Those protesters again!" she said. "That's what I was coming to tell you. The cops let all the people they arrested yesterday out of jail a couple of hours ago, and Joey showed up at the houseboat. The thing is, when he told me on the phone that he was wearing black when he was arrested, I assumed he was dressed like a mime. But when I saw him, he was wearing what looked a lot like what the protesters were wearing – black pants and a black T-shirt.”

“Does he often dress like that?” Mallory asked.

“No,” Sarah Willoughby said. “That’s the point. He usually wears white painters’ pants and really bright T-shirts, but I heard on the news that the men who kidnapped Adam Suleiman were dressed all in black. Joey's been very weird lately, very secretive and jittery – ”

She took a deep breath. “The minute I saw him, I jumped to the conclusion that he was one of the kidnappers – and I felt responsible.”

“But why?” asked Pete.

Sarah’s voice got thinner and higher. “Because he learned about the Suleimans' poems and the portfolio from me. I told him about them after I read about them in the paper. Usually he's so wrapped up in his own little world that he doesn't listen, but this really caught his attention.

“He wanted to know if maybe I had some legal claim on the English translations, since I was a direct descendant of the man who’d written them. I laughed and told him of course not – which seemed to disappoint him. When I saw what he was wearing when he got to the houseboat, I tried to call you and then drove up to the hostel."

As she began to turn around and go another way, the car was mobbed by black-clad figures, but she managed to back up. It was stop-and-go again, but at least they were making progress when suddenly, ahead of him in the crowd, Pete saw a guy on a souped-up motorbike wearing black leathers and a large black helmet with a black visor.

He tried to see the license plate, so he could check with Mallory about the number Bob had given her, but the bike was too far away and there were too many people and cars in between.

Still, Pete was sure it was David Wang. He was headed for a side street, and as Sarah's Subaru came to a stop once again, Pete saw Wang maneuver through the crowd, gun the bike, and take off at top speed.

"Did you see that guy?" Pete said to Mallory.

"Yes," she said tersely. "And it looks like he's going to get to the studio before we do. Do you think he's the kind of guy who might have a gun or something?"

"I don't know," Pete said. "All that leather. And that scar on his cheek probably means he was in a monster of a fight once. Even so, if he's on a motorbike, he can't be planning to take Adam somewhere. How's he going to get him on the bike?"

Pete was proud of how clearly he seemed to be thinking today – especially because, this time, Mallory immediately appreciated the significance of what he was saying.

"That's true!" she said. "Maybe he's just planning to check on Adam, to make sure he's O.K. Maybe Joey Barton moved Adam last night and maybe Wang's just bringing Adam food and water!"

Well, *maybe*, Pete thought. He supposed it was possible there was food and water in Wang's saddlebags. But as the traffic slowly cleared and Sarah was finally able to follow the motorbike down the side street, a darker set of thoughts came to Pete.

Sarah had said she wanted to kill Joey Barton. Of course, she'd simply meant she was very angry, but the comment had jolted Pete. And then Mallory had said Wang might have a gun. Maybe David Wang had threatened to kill Adam, and the reason Joey Barton had moved him was because he didn't want anything to do with killing! Maybe Barton hadn't told Wang he was moving Adam, but Wang had figured out where he'd been moved to, anyway — and now he was going there to take care of business.

Maybe he *did* have a gun, concealed somewhere in all that leather, or maybe a knife — and if he had either, and he got to Sarah Willoughby's studio before Sarah did, he could prove very dangerous. Pete knew it would be up to him to figure out how to take him on. Not that girls weren't brave — but they weren't as strong or fast as boys. That was the reason boys and girls never competed against one another in sports.

Pete looked around him in the Subaru to see if he could locate a weapon of some sort. He was happy to see a lug wrench lying next to the spare tire in the back. He grabbed it just as Sarah said, "That's my studio," and Mallory said, "And there's David Wang's bike!"

Pete looked up to see a simple building raised above the ground on piers, with an enormous deck surrounding it on all four sides. It did, indeed, look like the deck of a ship. The building itself was clad in weathered wood, with a slightly slanted roof, and two skylights that had been cranked wide open. There was no garage, but to one side of the building were some live oaks, and David Wang's bike had been parked there. Wang himself was nowhere to be seen.

Pete swallowed hard. "You should keep driving, Sarah," he said, "and let me out when you get around the corner. Or maybe all three of us should get out, and the two of you should see if you can jack up the bike somehow or put sand in the tank or something – so that he can't take off on it. I'll check out what's happening in the studio. And I think it's time to call the police."

"I do, too," Mallory said. "But with that mob of protesters in the way, it'll take them twenty minutes to get here, and that's if we're very, very lucky. I think Sarah and I should go with you to the studio."

"No," Pete said. "It's too dangerous. Besides, Wang would catch on quickly with three of us. I saw a second set of stairs to the deck at the back, where there aren't any windows. If I can get up there, I can see what's going on."

By that time, Sarah had pulled past her studio and out of sight. Pete knew that any more talk was useless. Now it was time to act.

Mallory turned to face him, looking worried. "Be careful," she said. "And good luck."

He nodded, grateful for her concern. Then he grabbed the lug wrench and hurried away from the car. Behind him, he could hear Sarah calling 911, but he knew Mallory had been right – with everything that was going on in Sausalito, it would be at least twenty minutes before the police arrived. It would be up to him.

As his grip tightened on the lug wrench, he could feel his pulse throbbing in his fingers. He realized he was breathing shallowly and quickly. He was tense, all right – or at least very keyed up – but also as determined as he'd ever felt in his life. He'd only met Adam once, but he'd liked him a lot, and Adam's absolute faith in The Three Investigators was what had brought them into this case to begin with. He wouldn't let Adam down.

Pete had no idea where David Wang was inside the studio. For all Pete knew, he could even now be opening the door to the kiln room where Adam was being kept. Maybe he should call out and distract Wang. Maybe he should just knock on the door innocently, and when Wang answered, he could hit him with the lug wrench. He groaned in frustration. The trouble was, he didn't know anything about Wang or how he might react, and he didn't know anything about the interior spaces of Sarah Willoughby's studio.

The house itself was odd, Pete thought – built as it was on a platform eight or nine feet off the ground. He'd seen pictures of houses like it, but they'd all been built near the ocean and had been raised to keep above hurricane storm surges that had destroyed so many coastal properties. This was at least a mile inland, and as far as he knew, there were never any hurricanes in San Francisco Bay.

As stealthily as he could, Pete snuck under the piers that held the house aloft. Above him David Wang was doing something. But what? Pete passed a rickety stepladder leaning against one of the piers just as he reached the stairs at the back of the house. Staying as low as possible, he crept up until he stood on the deck – a massive redwood collar surrounding the house. In the distance Richardson Bay glinted in the sun, and Pete could see sailboats cutting their way across the water. Overhead the sky was a solid blue bowl. He understood why the original builder had floated the house in the air.

Even so, he felt a little unmoored, as though he were actually on the deck of a ship. His heart was pounding now, and his legs felt a bit unsteady. He took a deep breath. It was at moments like this that he understood what true courage really was – not reckless wild abandon but the fortitude to go on in spite of fear and uncertainty.

He thought of Stephen Decatur and his attempt to retake the *Philadelphia*. Had he been frightened too? Who wouldn't have been? Pete wondered. Even if Decatur had sixty men under his command, he was facing the Barbary pirates who were not known for their courteous hospitality. He didn't know what lay ahead of him – on the one hand, success; on the other slavery or torture or death. But he went on with his mission.

Pete took heart from that, and from the fact that, though he didn't have sixty men to help him, at least David Wang wasn't a Barbary pirate.

With his back pressed against the house's siding, Pete cautiously sidestepped until he was next to the nearest window. It was a chance he felt he had to take. He swiveled, glanced through the glass, and then stepped away.

Wang was sitting in a straight-backed wooden chair in the middle of the room in a pillar of light. The livid scar on his cheek was startling. His right ankle rested on his left knee. In one hand was an opened can of beer and in the other a lit cigarette. So that's what had been in the saddlebags, Pete thought. No food and water for Adam. Now that Wang was here, he clearly felt he had all the time in the world.

Maybe he was thinking through his plan of how best to kill Adam. Or maybe just to move him. Adam had undoubtedly heard Wang come in, but he didn't know which of his kidnappers it was − the sadistic Wang or the more benevolent Joey Barton. He must be going crazy, Pete thought.

What to do? Pete's impulse was often to do the first thing that came to mind − which in this case was to break the window with the lug wrench and jump through. But he restrained himself. He was sure he'd get badly cut on the shards of glass, and anyway, if he did that, he'd give Wang plenty of time to be on his feet to meet him. No, what was needed was surprise.

He closed his eyes and took several deep breaths to calm himself. He thought of Stephen Decatur boarding the *Philadelphia* under cover of darkness, creeping along the deck, dropping down into the hold −

Wait a minute, Pete thought. The chair Wang was sitting in was directly underneath one of the roof's two skylights. If Pete could get up there, maybe he could –

He crept sideways, away from the window, toward the windowless back of the house. To his great excitement he found a folding wooden deck chair that he could stand on. Though Sarah had boarded over the windows in the back, the sills were still there, jutting out. If he could stand on the sill, maybe he could reach high enough to get a purchase on the roof. Maybe all the pull-ups he'd done would come in handy now.

Cautiously he climbed on the chair and stepped from it to the sill. He almost lost his balance as he reached up, and slightly backwards, to the overhanging roof. Pete found that the builders had fashioned a metal lip on the edge to sluice water away during the short rainy season. Maybe it would hold him. But he'd need two hands.

He shoved the lug wrench in the back of his pants where the metal was cold and hard against his skin, uncomfortable and awkward to boot. Then he gripped the roof's lip, hopped upward, and pulled. He found himself hanging, his biceps straining. He inched up, grunting, but even as he did, he realized that he'd never be able to get his knee or leg up on the roof itself. If only there was a ladder – .

He dropped to the deck and slapped himself on the forehead with the heel of his hand. What a doofus he could be! He began to move fast. Stealthy as a cat, he crept down the stairs, grabbed the stepladder he'd barely noticed earlier, then hurried back up and positioned it under the eaves.

The ladder was old and made of wood and clearly had seen better days. As Pete set it up, he remembered his father saying many times that you never climbed all the way up a stepladder, never *ever* stood on the top step. Pete was sorry to disobey his father, but today he had no choice. The ladder swayed as he climbed, one step after another, until he was grasping the very top step. From here it would all be a matter of balance. Carefully he climbed one step and then another until there was nothing left but to take the last and final step. With nothing to hold onto but the air, Pete put one of his feet on the top step and then brought the other one up to join it.

The whole thing felt so precarious, he was sure it was about to topple him to the ground, but he jumped and landed part way on the roof. He winced as the ladder toppled to the deck with a loud clatter. Uh oh, Pete thought. Wang must have heard that. He scrabbled upwards on the roof's asphalt shingles, away from the eaves, making himself as flat as he could.

The front door of the house banged open and Pete heard footsteps. "Who's there?" a voice called, and Pete took heart at what he thought was a touch of panic. He crawled toward the nearer skylight and peered down. Wang, seeing no one on the deck, had gone back inside. Now he stood where he'd been sitting before, right under the skylight that had been cranked open as far as it would go. As he looked down, Pete saw that Wang had taken a black balaclava out of his pocket and was wrestling it over his head. He was going to try to move Adam, then – who must never have seen his face.

Pete jumped to his feet and positioned himself on the open side of the skylight. He cocked his leg and kicked as hard as he could with his heel against the raised edge. The force broke the skylight's hinges and sent it flying. Without another thought, Pete grabbed the lug wrench from his pants, stepped forward, and dropped through the opening in the roof, right onto David Wang.

They sprawled on the floor, both of them stunned. The lug wrench went flying. Pete was amazed to find he hadn't badly injured himself – but then he'd had the luxury of having his fall broken by a human body. Wang hadn't been so lucky. He groaned as he staggered to his feet and limped toward Pete.

"Who the hell are you?" Wang growled. Though the scar had made him look dangerous, the balaclava was downright frightening. He lunged at Pete, who sidestepped. He found himself backing against one of the walls lined with wooden shelves on which Sarah Willoughby had placed some of her finished pots. Pete kicked out at Wang who made a move to grab his foot and upend him. When Wang fished in his pocket and took out a knife, Pete knew he had to act fast.

From behind him on the shelf, he grabbed a clay pot by the lip and hurled it at Wang. Wang dropped the knife in order to parry what Pete had thrown, and as he stooped to retrieve it, Pete grabbed another pot, this one even bigger and heavier. In a sweeping arc, he brought it down hard on David Wang's skull.

The man fell to the floor with a thud and stayed there.

For a moment Pete just stood where he was, breathing hard. His shoulder hurt where he'd fallen on it. He was shaking with adrenaline. But he was in better shape than David Wang. A trickle of blood ran from Wang's scalp onto the wooden floor.

Pete searched for and found the lug wrench he'd dropped when he jumped. He picked it up and rushed to the locked door at the back of the building. "Adam!" he called. "It's Pete Crenshaw! Just a minute!"

"Pete!" Adam's muffled voice called.

Fueled by the adrenaline, Pete swung the lug wrench at the padlock, and the whole thing came away – the lock and the hasp that had held it. They clattered to the floor as Pete swung open the door. There stood Adam Suleiman, blinking in the sudden glare, looking pale and frightened. He grabbed Pete's hands and clung to them as though they were a life raft.

"I knew –," he said. "I knew you'd come."

Behind him, Pete heard the door open and Mallory and Sarah Willoughby rush in. Mallory's gaze swept from Pete to the body on the floor to Adam.

"Pete!" she said. "When we saw you jump through the roof – . Adam, are you O.K.?"

"Yes," he said, "I am. Thanks to Pete

and The Three Investigators."

Outside, Pete heard the sound of sirens. He went to the window where two cruisers, their lights flashing, skidded to a stop. Sausalito's finest, Pete thought. And better late than never. At least they could arrest David Wang. And boy, did he have a story to tell! It was such a great story, he was even going to tell it to his mother! And Califia Garcia-Wiliams!

Of course, it was too bad that he and the other Three Investigators hadn't been able to solve the mystery of what had been in the secret pocket of the portfolio – and who had taken it, then left it in Grace Cathedral. But even though Adam had been hoping they could do that, Pete was sure that even *Adam* would agree that the mystery they *had* solved – the mystery of who had taken Adam and where they were keeping him! – was a lot more important than the one Adam had called them in on to begin with.

But Pete found out almost at once that he was wrong. As they all went toward the police cruisers, Adam said to him and Mallory, "It really *was* scary to be kidnapped. But the worst part was that I was afraid my father would cave in and give them what they wanted.

If he'd done that, not only would the de Boissy poems have been lost forever, but you and Bob and Jupiter would never have been able to figure why they'd been stolen to begin with!"

15

A Labyrinthian Legacy

Three days later, Jupiter sat in the outdoor workshop of the Salvage Yard waiting for Pete, Bob, and Mallory. He could hardly have been more pleased with how well the last case of the season had panned out. Both David Wang and Joey Barton were in jail at the moment, but it seemed likely that Barton would be making a deal with the authorities in which he testified against Wang in exchange for a reduced sentence, or probation.

According to Sarah Willoughby – who'd visited Barton in jail – he'd told the police that once he'd helped David Wang kidnap Adam and lock him in Wang's shed, he'd started to feel queasy about what he'd done – especially after Wang had suddenly told him that they might be better off "disposing of" Adam once they had the poems.

Barton hadn't known if Wang was serious, but he'd found the suggestion so chilling that when Wang had had to stay with his son in Alameda the night after the kidnapping, he'd decided to get Adam away from David Wang's shed and hide him in Sarah Willoughby's studio until he could figure out what to do next.

He and David Wang had discussed the studio as a possible hiding place right from the start. He'd stocked the kiln room with plenty of food and water, as well as an old army cot, then got Adam there and told him he'd be back in the morning. Unfortunately, as he'd made his way from the studio to the houseboat, he'd been swept up in the arrest of the protesters.

In the meanwhile, although Wang had been counting on Barton to take care of Adam while he was away in Alameda, he wanted to check things out for himself when he could. His route with California Bounty started early. When he'd gotten to the farmers' market in Danville, his last stop of the day, he'd convinced an acquaintance to watch the truck while he went to check on Adam. Finding Adam gone, he'd retrieved the truck, dropped it at his house, and headed straight for Sarah Willoughby's studio on his bike.

Wang wasn't talking, but Jupiter assumed that his plan had been to take Adam out of the studio and put him somewhere else before Barton was released from jail. It probably hadn't even occurred to him that it was broad daylight and that his only vehicle was a motorcycle until after he arrived at the potter's work-shop.

Although Jupiter had known for a long time now that most criminals were hardly the sharpest tacks in the box, he still found David Wang's actions that day amazingly dimwitted. Jupiter also thought that Wang could not have *actually* intended to kill Adam or he would hardly have been drinking a beer and smoking a cigarette when Pete dropped through the sky-light directly onto his head.

In any case, one of the most surprising parts about the wrap-up came when Adam learned the identity of the kidnappers. He'd been astonished that one of them was the fa-ther of a classmate of his; as it happened, Adam went to school with David Wang's son.

"His name is Jesse," Adam had told Ju-piter and the others. "I can't remember whether I told you this the day you came to my house, but I talked to some friends at school about your website and said I'd called you in about the poems. I didn't tell Jesse himself about the portfolio being stolen, but I told a friend who knows Jesse pretty well, and I bet he mentioned it to him."

"Wow!" Pete had said. "I wonder if that had anything to do with what happened?"

"Possibly," Jupiter had said. "Maybe David Wang heard about us being called onto the case even before he decided to get involved in the kidnapping. As it turns out," he'd explained to Adam, "Wang used to work for a real estate developer in Auburn, and he lost his job – and potentially a lot of money – when Bob, Pete, Mallory, and I prevented his boss from taking a bag of gold that belonged to someone else."

By this time, Adam had been staring at him open-mouthed.

"You mean David Wang was involved in the first Auburn case?" he asked in amazement.

Adam had looked as if the world were turning under him, and Jupiter too had had a vertiginous feeling. He'd never before met anyone who'd read Bob's case reports without knowing The Three Investigators personally, and it was strange to consider that to someone like Adam, they had simply seemed like characters in a story until he'd met them. Bob had been careful to conceal the identities of most of the people they met in their cases, but he'd used the real names of The Three Investigators and Mallory in his case reports.

Still, while Adam had loved what he now

thought of as *The Mystery of the Abecedarian Academy*, David Wang would have been a lot less pleased with it, Jupiter thought.

In fact, if David Wang had learned, from an overheard conversation in the kitchen of the Tri-Faith Center, that some religious poems were worth a lot of money, and afterwards had been told by his son that a boy named Adam Suleiman had called in The Three Investigators on a case involving those poems, he might well have decided to kidnap Adam, not merely for the money, but also to get revenge on the four people he'd described to Joey Barton as "young jerks."

"Of course, his main motive was the money," Jupiter had said, "but Wang must have also really hated us after what happened last summer. He must have jumped at the chance to get back at us."

"But in the end it was Pete who jumped *him*!" Adam had said proudly. "I didn't see it happen, but I heard it, and I saw David Wang afterwards. On the floor. Surrounded by a lot of pottery shards!"

"Geez!" said Pete. "If I'd known he hated me, personally, I might have been a lot more scared. As it was, I just imagined that I was Stephen Decatur on the deck of the *Phila-*

delphia after it was captured by the Barbary pirates!"

Still, to Jupiter, the most satisfactory thing about the whole case had been the expressions on his friends' faces when – not long after they'd returned to the hostel from Sarah Willoughy's studio where Adam and his father had been reunited – he'd told them what he'd deduced about the theft and return of the portfolio.

By then, Jupiter had felt certain for some time that Father Samuel was keeping a pretty big secret, but it was only when he was driving Bob and Jupiter back from Danville that Jupiter had finally figured out what the secret was.

He'd had a clue right from the beginning, but he hadn't paid enough attention to it. When the four of them had gone to Grace Cathedral and Jupiter had met the cleaning woman, she'd told him that the day she'd discovered the portfolio there'd been an ecumenical service attended by a lot of imams and rabbis and ministers and priests. Priests like Father Samuel.

Jupiter didn't know why this hadn't occurred to him earlier; after all, he'd known from the time Father Samuel had first shown up in the Salvage Yard that he'd known the

Suleiman family in Morocco, and just recently Father Samuel had revealed that he'd had access to the library there and had read the poems many years ago.

It had suddenly seemed to him likely that when Father Samuel had first examined the portfolio, he'd discovered the contents of its secret pocket – and, almost certainly, after examining whatever it was, had put it back. He'd known it was there for twenty-odd years and had had no problem with it staying where it was. But after Adam and his father had decided to donate the poems to the Tri-Faith Center, Father Samuel had examined the secret pocket again and this time had removed whatever had been inside it.

"But what could that be?" Pete had asked.

"I have no idea," Jupiter had said. "But when we see Father Samuel tomorrow, I'm going to ask him."

He had, too – when the four of them and Father Samuel were all back at the Suleiman house the day after Adam was rescued. Adam had been explaining that Barton and Wang had always worn black balaclavas when they were around him and had never said anything that would have let him guess their identities – at least not until Barton said he was taking Adam to the potter's studio, and Adam had managed to write the reference to Isaiah 64:8.

"I'm so glad it all worked out," said Father Samuel. "I felt so guilty – so very, very guilty, because – well, because – "

"Because what you told me about the portfolio the day you came to the Salvage Yard wasn't strictly true, was it?" Jupiter had asked gently.

His question had opened the floodgates, and the whole story had come pouring out. When Father Samuel had been in Morocco all those years before and had discovered the portfolio in the Suleiman family's library, he had noticed that the back cover was made of two pieces of leather sewn together, and was, effectively, a pocket.

After reading the twelve de Boissy villanelles, he'd been in a state of awe and had hoped more poems might be hidden in that pocket. But when he opened it, he discovered a thirteenth villanelle – one written much later than the others, at the very end of de Boissy's life.

"Imagine my shock to find that it was totally unlike the others," Father Samuel had said. "It seemed de Boissy's faith in almighty

God had been badly shaken. The thirteenth poem was a cry of defiance and anger. If God were indeed almighty, why hadn't he stopped the Protestant Reformation? In England, monasteries and convents were being burned and priests and nuns executed. How could God have allowed that to happen? De Boissy had written a very dark coda to his earlier poems of faith and light and beauty."

Here, Father Samuel had stopped and shaken his head mournfully, unable to meet the eyes of the Suleimans. But eventually he continued.

"De Boissy's family had sent the thirteenth poem to the Pope along with the other twelve, but they'd hidden it in the secret pocket together with a letter explaining that they really didn't want the world to know about it. They were afraid it would completely shatter the image of Jacques de Boissy as both a great poet and a committed and reverent Catholic.

"As the letter put it," Father Samuel continued, "they left it up to God. If the Pope found the poem and read it, so be it. But if he didn't, then when he returned the portfolio to the family, no one would be the wiser, and that, too, would have been meant to be. Which might have happened if it hadn't been for the

Barbary pirates. Anyway, although I was shaken to find it, I put it back – stitching the portfolio up with some silk thread I'd purchased at the local souk.

"All these years, I've known it was there, but I wouldn't have done anything about it if Jacob hadn't decided to give the portfolio to the Tri-Faith Center. I knew that any conservator worth his salt would immediately spy the modern thread and find the thirteenth poem. And then the whole world would know that de Boissy had lost his faith in God. I gave in to the impulse of a moment, and I've been regretting it ever since."

That had been quite a moment, Jupiter reflected.

After Adam and Jacob Suleiman had gotten over their initial shock at the revelation, Father Samuel had begged them to forgive him. Then the old priest had taken an archival envelope containing the thirteenth villanelle and the letter the de Boissy family had written to the Pope out of his cassock pocket and handed them to Adam.

Adam had been the first to read the thirteenth poem. "It's very sad," he said. "I'm so sorry de Boissy felt that way at the end of his life. I hope he regained his belief in God's goodness before he died."

Before they'd left the Suleiman house, Adam had given them a present to serve as their case memento, and it was a stunner. He'd run into the house and returned carrying the drawing of the labyrinth at Chartres that Jupiter had seen on the wall of his bedroom.

"I told you a French artist did this drawing," Adam had said, holding it up for everyone to see, "but I didn't tell you I designed its frame. The wooden rosettes at the four corners were carved by a local craftsman." Now, the drawing was in Three Investigators Headquarters, leaning against a wall and waiting to be hung.

Just then, Jupiter heard voices, and soon Pete, Bob, and Mallory were joining him in the outdoor workshop. Under her arm, Mallory was carrying a sheaf of papers.

"Well, I'm done," she said. "At least I hope so. The plans for our new Headquarters. Which Jacob Suleiman is going to help me to whip into final shape. The two of us are going to figure out how to put a new roof on my favorite shed. My main idea was to raise the ceiling, and the roof, to let a lot of light in. Here," she added, thrusting the sheaf of papers at Jupiter. "You can see the basic design on the top drawing. I've sent a copy of my plans to Jacob, and he's going to turn them into real blueprints on his architectural computer program," Mallory added. "That way we'll have professional drawings. It'll take a few weeks, so for now you'll have to be satisfied with these."

And Jupiter *was* satisfied. From what he could see, Mallory had done a terrific job of re-imagining the shed as a place where they could meet with clients but also hang out with one another. He was glad he so fully approved of the drawings and the plan. He wasn't good at faking his feelings, and it was a great relief to know he didn't have to.

"So," Mallory said, "we've got a new Headquarters on the way, and a perfect memento for our last case. But what about a title? Have you figured one out yet, Bob?"

"Sort of, but not completely," Bob said. "I mean, since this case will be LL and there's a labyrinth in it — well, *three* labyrinths, really — it seems as if I should be able to come up with an L adjective which would work. But so far I can't. I thought of liturgical, because of the church and Father Samuel, and lexical, because of the poem, but I'm not sure what either of them would *mean*. Maybe because I'm not sure what this case meant to *me*. What about you guys? What stood out most strongly for you?"

"How dangerous San Francisco has gotten, as much as anything else," Pete said. "And also the Barbary pirates and Stephen Decatur and the *Philadelphia*. And that protest group acting so wacko about the monument to the war dead."

"To me it was about staying in a hostel that had once been a military hospital," said Mallory, "and seeing an architect living in a house he'd designed himself. And visiting Hiroka on her houseboat. What about you, Bob?"

Bob looked a little embarrassed. "I have to admit that, to me, it was partly about Adam Suleiman wanting us on the case because of my reports. Though also about David Wang wanting to get The Three Investigators because of something we'd done to him last summer."

"Yeah, that was way weird," said Pete. "What about you, Jupe?" he asked.

Jupiter thought for a moment. "Well, I agree with everything all of you have mentioned," he said. But ever since I started reading that book of essays about human achievements through the ages, I've been thinking that since a lot of them were created in order to honor gods, maybe religion played a much bigger role in creating what we now call 'civilization' than I'd previously considered."

"You thought about that when we were up north?" Pete asked.

"I basically had to," Jupiter said. "It was one thing to read about what had happened to San Francisco and another thing to see it in person. Father Samuel was right when he'd said that the city had fallen on hard times – that it seemed a hotbed of chaos these days. I mean, chaos and order are both legacies of human life, but if cities become chaotic, anarchy breaks out. It's scary to see it happen – and even scarier to think that people are letting it."

"How about legacy, then?" Mallory asked. "It's an L word, and if Bob just changed 'labyrinth' to its adjective form, he'd have a title that would work."

"So the Labyrinthian Legacy would be the legacy of religion?" Bob asked.

"Not exactly," Mallory said. "There are a lot of moments in human history when order wrestled with chaos, and order won. And we've seen a bunch of them this summer. The legacy of Galileo and the Greeks. The legacy of the written word. The legacy of Native Americans and Wiccans and the Christian church. All the legacies our species has inherited from past ages. It would be more like the fact that villanelles and cathedrals and formal labyrinths and navies are all orderly conceptions that can be handed down from one generation to the next – while chaos is just chaos.”

“I totally get it,” Bob said. “And it actually goes along with something I wrote about after the Galilean grindstone case. Scientists and religious people can look pretty different from the outside, but religious orders are called ‘orders’ for a reason! And the word ‘labyrinthian’ doesn’t mean chaotic or confusing – just complex!”

They all looked at one another and grinned, and then Pete jumped to his feet. “I’m going to get us all sodas,” he said.

When he came back, for a while they sat in the outdoor workshop drinking – all of them, apparently, feeling happy, but Jupiter, Pete, and Bob occasionally grinning at one another in anticipation. Until Jupiter decided it was time for him, Pete, and Bob to give Mallory her end-of-the-season gifts. At Jupiter’s nod, Bob jumped to his feet, opened Easy Three, went into HQ1, and returned with three packages.

Though they’d taken the packages north with them, there’d never been a proper moment to present them to Mallory. The day after they'd rescued Adam, Jacob had driven the four of them and Adam to Grace Cathedral for a final visit to the labyrinth, and that evening Adam had hosted them, and Hiroka Ito, at a Moroccan meal ordered from the fanciest Moroccan restaurant in San Francisco but eaten in the Golden Gate Hostel.

Adam had wanted to see the hostel, anyway, and Mallory had said she thought it would be easier to convince Hiroka to join them if she just had to go the short distance from her parents' houseboat rather than all the way to a stranger's house in Alameda.

And although for a while Jupiter had thought that he and the others might have time to give Mallory her presents at the hostel, it just hadn't worked out. Besides, it was more fitting that she open them here, in the Salvage Yard.

Mallory sat stunned as Bob handed the packages to her.

"What are these?" she asked.

"Open them," Pete said.

But before she'd gotten very far, Jupiter found himself nervously talking. "I hope you like the color," he said. "If you don't, we can always exchange it for something else."

Mallory was paying little attention. She

unwrapped the smallest box first and exclaimed in delight.

"My own chalk!" she said. "And you found it in teal! How did you know teal was my favorite color?"

"Jupiter's observation," said Pete. "Open the big one next."

When she'd unwrapped the bicycle helmet, she grinned and put it on. Pete and Bob started hooting, and Jupiter could see, right off, that the color was a success. The blue-green of the helmet looked great with Mallory's red hair and blue eyes – and as he watched her stride over to Easy Three, he could hardly believe how pretty she was.

At Easy Three, she took her chalk and carefully drew three question marks on the door. Three question marks in a certain color were proof positive that a specific member of The Three Investigators had drawn the marks, and the last time the four of them had seen marks like these was at the end of the previous case.

When Mallory returned to the outside workshop and sat down again, Jupiter handed her the third and final box. He watched as she tore the paper off, removed the plain white cover, and stared at a tidy stack of new Three

Investigators business cards. She took one out and held it in her hand. It read:

THE THREE INVESTIGATORS
"We Investigate Anything"
???
First Investigator – Jupiter Jones
Second Investigator – Pete Crenshaw
Records and Research – Bob Andrews
Special Consultant – Mallory MacLeod

Jupiter's name was in red, Pete's in dark sky blue, Bob's in yellow-green, and Mallory's in teal. As she took a card in her hand and stared at it, almost in awe, Bob and Pete both said "I hope you like them!"– to which Mallory said, "Oh, man, do I ever!" Then she put her palms to her cheeks as if she suddenly felt hot.

Jupiter had noticed that, although Mallory was an excellent actress when she set out to be one, she wasn't good at faking her feelings. That was something else they had in common, he thought with sudden satisfaction. He grabbed a piece of teal-colored chalk and strode over to Easy Three. In front of him were the three question marks Mallory had drawn. He reached up and drew a fourth one next to them. Pete and Bob both cheered, and Mallory looked happier than Jupiter had ever seen her.

Soon, Pete, Bob, and Mallory were saying goodbye – heading for their bikes and then for their homes – but Jupiter sat for a while longer in the outdoor workshop, looking at the question marks. It had been a good case with which to end the summer. Bob had gotten what he'd wanted and deserved for quite some time now – a case that had come to The Three Investigators because of his excellent writing. Pete had acted with amazing bravery in leaping through the skylight as if he were leaping into the hold of a ship held by Barbary pirates. And Mallory had taken the opportunity presented by their meeting with Jacob Suleiman to ask a real architect to help finalize her plans for a new Three Investigators headquarters.

As for his own experience, Jupiter was happy that his instinct about Father Samuel's secret had proved correct. Describing yourself could be a very difficult task, but ever since he could remember, Jupiter had known he was different from most other people. If comparing and contrasting two things that might seem, on the surface, to have little in common really *was* the fundamental business of the human mind, then he had started off on that business quite young. Although he'd never said this aloud to anyone, from his earliest childhood he'd felt he had a special destiny, a destiny that required seeing the other members of his own species at a certain – and sometimes strange – remove.

But while it was true that he could seem stoical and put thinking ahead of feeling, that didn't mean he lacked emotion. In fact, he felt things very keenly. He wasn't a loner – he was a leader and collaborator – and as the long, hot southern California summer came to its natural end, he was amazed at how much The Three Investigators had already accomplished, and how much they might still accomplish in the future.

ABOUT THE AUTHORS

Elizabeth Arthur

Elizabeth was born on November 15, 1953 in New York City. She is the daughter of Robert Arthur, the creator of The Three Investigators series. She was educated at Concord Academy in Concord, Massachusetts, the University of Michigan in Ann Arbor, Michigan, Notre Dame University of Nelson, British Columbia, and the University of Victoria in Victoria, British Columbia.

Before she started working on the New Three Investigators series in December of 2018, Elizabeth spent most of her life writing for adults. *Island Sojourn* – a memoir about building a house on a wilderness island in northern Canada – was published in 1980 by Harper and Row. A second memoir, *Looking For The Klondike Stone*, was published by Knopf in 1992. She is also the author of the novels *Beyond the Mountain, Bad Guys, Binding Spell, Antarctic Navigation*, and *Bring Deeps*.

Elizabeth's writing has received fellowships, grants, and awards from the Bread Loaf Writer's Conference, the Ossabaw Island Project, the Vermont Council on the Arts, and the

Indiana Arts Commission. She twice received fellowships from the National Endowment for the Arts and was the first novelist ever given an Antarctic Artists and Writers Operational Support Grant from the National Science Foundation.

Her novel *Antarctic Navigation* was chosen by the New York *Times* as a Notable Book, received a Critics' Choice Award from the San Francisco *Review of Books*, and was chosen as a Best Book of 1995 by *A Common Reader*. In 1996 the novel received the Ohioana Book Award for Fiction from the Ohioana Library Association.

Elizabeth has also taught creative writing at Miami University in Oxford, Ohio; the University of Cincinnati; and Indiana University/Purdue University of Indianapolis, where she directed the creative writing program. She and Steven Bauer met in 1980 at the Bread Loaf Writer's Conference and have been married since June of 1982.

Steven Bauer

Steven was born on September 10, 1948 in Newark, New Jersey. He was educated at Hanover Park High School in East Hanover, New Jersey, Trinity College in Hartford, Connecticut, and the University of Massachusetts in Amherst, Massachusetts. In 1970 he received a **B.A.** with Honors in English from Trinity, and in 1975 he received an **M.F.A.** in English from the University of Massachusetts.

Steven is the author of three books for young people – *Satyrday*, 1980; *The Strange and Wonderful Tale of Robert McDoodle*, 1999; and *A Cat of a Different Color*, 2000. His book of poems *Daylight Savings* was published by Gibbs Smith in 1989 and won the Peregrine Smith Poetry Prize.

Steven's work has received fellowships from the Bread Loaf Writer's Conference and the Fine Arts Work Center in Provincetown, Massachusetts. In addition, he has been given grants and awards from the American Library Association, the Parents' Choice Foundation, the Ossabaw Island Project, the Massachusetts Arts Council, and the Indiana Arts Commission.

From 1979 to 1982, Steven taught literature and creative writing at Colby College in Waterville, Maine. From 1982 to 2009 he taught at Miami University in Oxford, Ohio where he directed the graduate and under-graduate creative writing programs. In 2010 he established Hollow Tree Literary Services, an independent editing business.